TOO MANY INTERESTING
THINGS ARE HAPPENING TO

ETHAN
FAIRMONT

TOO MANY INTERESTING
THINGS ARE HAPPENING TO

ETHAN FAIRMONT

NICK BROOKS

union
square
kids

NEW YORK

union
square
kids

NEW YORK

UNION SQUARE KIDS and the distinctive Union Square Kids logo
are trademarks of Union Square & Co., LLC.

Union Square & Co., LLC, is a subsidiary of Sterling Publishing Co., Inc.

ISBN 978-1-60582-331-7 (galley)
ISBN 978-1-4549-4710-3 (hardcover)
ISBN 978-1-4549-4711-0 (paperback)
ISBN 978-1-4549-4712-7 (e-book)

Library of Congress Cataloging-in-Publication Data

Names: Brooks, Nick, author.
Title: Too many interesting things are happening to Ethan Fairmont / Nick Brooks.
Description: New York : Union Square Kids, 2023. | Series: Ethan Fairmont ; book 2 |
    Audience: Ages 8-12. | Audience: Grades 4-6. | Summary: "Ethan Fairmont and his
    friends attempt intergalactic communication and discover danger lurking close to home"—
    Provided by publisher.
Identifiers: LCCN 2022036779 (print) | LCCN 2022036780 (ebook) | ISBN 9781454947103
    (hardcover) | ISBN 9781454947110 (paperback) | ISBN 9781454947127 (epub)
Subjects: CYAC: Extraterrestrial beings—Fiction. | Friendship—Fiction. |
    Schools—Fiction. | Family life—Fiction. | African Americans—Fiction. |
    Science fiction. | LCGFT: Science fiction. | Novels.
Classification: LCC PZ7.1.B76154 To 2023 (print) | LCC PZ7.1.B76154 (ebook) |
    DDC [Fic]—dc23
LC record available at https://lccn.loc.gov/2022036779
LC ebook record available at https://lccn.loc.gov/2022036780

For information about custom editions, special sales, and premium purchases,
please contact specialsales@unionsquareandco.com.

Printed in Canada

Lot #:
2 4 6 8 10 9 7 5 3 1
04/23

unionsquareandco.com

Created in association with Cake Creative LLC

Cover illustration by Khadijah Khatib

Dedicated to Troi + Tyson

NEW BEGINNINGS

The problem with guinea pigs is that they don't respect the rules.

"Nugget!" I called, my voice echoing in the emptiness of the Create Space. He didn't answer, of course—he's a guinea pig. But he didn't make any other sounds, either: no scratching or scrabbling to help me track him down. I grumbled to myself as I searched under all the chairs. "You know the rules. You stay in your pen when we're here!"

I don't know about other guinea pigs, but Nugget is very social. Most pets would have wigged out after everything that happened over the summer. You know, new friends and visiting aliens, but not Nugget. Nugget enjoyed new things, so I'd been bringing him to the Create Space that I opened with Juan Carlos and Kareem.

The Create Space was designed to be a sanctuary for all the scientists and inventors and imaginators who didn't have a place to call home. I was fortunate to have the abandoned factory as my personal sanctuary, but I was being selfish keeping it all to myself. So, with money our family received from the police department—after they wrongfully accused my dad of harboring a criminal and wrestled and cuffed him on our front lawn—we turned the factory into a functioning learning center.

On both sides of the floor we put up shelves and stocked them with science, engineering, and math books. We had smaller office rooms toward the back of the space where kids could work on projects or read in a quiet space. And, in the center, we had rows of computers for friends to use as they pleased.

We opened every day after school and any kid in the neighborhood could come as much as they wanted, or at least until the streetlights came on and I had to close up shop.

The first few weeks were slow, so I figured I'd bring Nugget to keep us company. It had been fine until this week. Somehow, Nugget figured out how to lift the door of his cage and escape. Today I closed the door with a bread tie and Nugget chewed right through it and escaped anyway!

"Nugget!" I called in a sterner voice. "This is getting ridiculous!"

"Have you found him yet?" Kareem called, emerging from the bathroom drying his hands.

"No," I groaned. "I can't believe he's pulling this game when he knows I need to get home and get ready for the first day of school."

"Um, does he *really* know that?" Kareem said. "Nugget is a guinea pig."

"Oh, he knows," I glowered. "This is all part of his twisted sense of humor."

Kareem shook his head.

"Well, I would stay and help you look for him, but my dad says I have to get some last-minute stuff for school."

Juan Carlos would usually be here with us, but he had to get stuff for school, too. He and Kareem both like to wait until the last minute for things. I must be the only one excited about school because I've been prepared for weeks.

"No worries," I said, peering under the bright orange thinking couch. "I'm going to eat a granola bar in a second and that will lure him out."

Kareem walked toward the door, laughing, but all of a sudden the laugh turned into a yelp and he dove down low to the floor.

"Ethan, duck! Quick! Before he sees you!"

I flung myself to the ground, my heart thumping. I immediately had flashbacks from the summer, remembering the Others and their hunt for Cheese.

"What is it? What's going on?" I whispered.

"That dude," he hissed. "Jodie!"

Kareem was close to the door, and he crawled over to it, reaching up to lock the entrance to the Create Space.

"Jodie?" I whispered. Then I remembered. "Oh, the new kid? The alien kid?"

"Yes," he groaned quietly. "He's coming right this way."

I hid under a table, and, sure enough, a moment later I heard the sound of the entrance rattling as Jodie tried the knob.

"What does he want?" I said.

"To ask me a million questions," Kareem sighed. "Or you. He says he's starting some new group when school starts—for *alien enthusiasts*."

My heart started thumping again. Jodie had showed up at the Create Space a few weeks back, asking questions about aliens. I never remember his name. In my head I just call him *Guy to Stay Away From*. At first, he seemed normal and like he just wanted to be part of the Create Space community. But then he started asking questions about aliens. Too many questions. Did we believe in them? Had we ever seen one? Did we think they'd ever come to Ferrous City? I'd always made sure to be busy when he stopped by, and I hadn't seen him in a while. I thought he'd given up. But it looks like I was wrong.

"You don't think he knows anything, do you?" I whispered to Kareem.

"No, I don't think so. How would he?" Kareem answered, pressed against the door. I'm glad the windows of the building are too high for Jodie to peek through. "I've heard him asking other people the same questions. He's fixated on this building for some reason, but I don't think it's *us*."

"Is he gone?" I whispered when it went silent.

Kareem slowly stood up and then peeked through the peephole.

"Looks like it. My dad is going to be here any minute. Are you going to lock up?"

"Yeah, I've got it."

"Okay, well . . . I'll see you in school tomorrow. Ugh. *School. Tomorrow.*"

I grinned a wide obnoxious grin, and Kareem sucked his teeth.

"Peace," he grunted.

"Peace."

With Kareem gone, the place felt even emptier. Even though I was glad that Jodie hadn't come in, just thinking about him and his questions made me feel lonely. Time had passed. Things are supposed to get easier with time. But even though I was busy and life was fun at the Create Space, I really missed Cheese.

I didn't bother to stand up. I reached into my pocket, pulled out the granola bar and unwrapped it slowly, thinking about everything that happened this summer. I got Kareem back as a friend. But I had to say goodbye to Cheese. It had only been two months, though it seemed like forever.

I'd taken two bites of the granola bar when I heard a scratching sound coming from the orange thinking couch. I looked under it in my search for Nugget, but the cushions on top wiggled. A moment later he appeared, his beady black eyes shining.

"Go figure," I muttered, and took another bite.

Nugget beelined across the floor of the old factory to my lap, where he climbed up on my shoe and paused. I offered him a piece of the granola bar and we both sat there silently eating.

When the Create Space was full of people doing experiments and building stuff, it was easy to be distracted and not think about what had happened in this place—the things that only me and Kareem and Juan Carlos and the Others knew about. But when it was empty, it felt the same as lying in bed at night. Wondering where in the galaxy Cheese was. Wondering if my friend was happy and safe.

I gave Nugget the last bite of the granola bar, trying not to be too sad. At least the thought of school starting tomorrow was exciting. Maybe it would be just the distraction I needed.

2

THE NEWCOMER

I could understand why some people wouldn't be excited about the first day of school. Not everybody likes being around new people—or even the old people they know are going to be there. Maybe if Juan Carlos and Kareem weren't going to be in my science block, I would be dragging my feet on the way to school. But knowing they'd be there made me feel like I was flying as I walked the eight blocks.

Plus, I'm a sixth grader now. That means I finally get to have Ms. Erivo for science, which I've been looking forward to since third grade. The older kids always talked about how cool her classroom is and how she does lots of projects. I smiled as I climbed the steps to the school. Kareem hates projects. But I'd make sure we get paired for it and then he wouldn't hate it so much.

When I stepped inside the school, it looked like a typical first day. Everybody had new shoes, new backpacks, new clothes, new everything. I never really needed to buy clothes. With two big brothers, every year I had a fresh new wardrobe. Well, new to me at least. They had a way cooler style than I ever did so I didn't mind getting their hand-me-downs. But shoes were something different. By the time I could fit into my big brothers' shoes, they were already a little too worn for back-to-school material. Everybody, no matter who you were, sported brand-new kicks on the first day of school. Walking through the halls toward my locker, I noticed Jordans, Vans, Nikes, Chucks, all of them sparkling new. Even Juan Carlos, who was positive his abuela wouldn't get him a new pair of kicks, was wearing some brand-new Adidas.

Juan Carlos wasn't smiling as I walked up to him. I felt my stomach sink. Even after the time that has passed, I still got worried when he or Kareem were worried. My first thought was always *Did something happen to Cheese?* Then I'd remind myself that Cheese was long gone, and my stomach would sink even lower.

"What's wrong?" I asked when I reached him. He stood by his locker, looking deflated.

"I got here early so I could make sure I got my locker open," he said. "And it didn't even matter. I'm never going to get this thing open!"

"You have your combination?"

Looking miserable, he handed me the slip of paper he'd been squinting at. It was kind of damp from his sweaty palm. Gross. I held it by the corner and peered at it.

"1-11-9," he groaned. "I've done it over and over."

I reached for the lock on his locker and tried the combination. No luck. Then something occurred to me. I flipped the piece of paper upside down. Juan Carlos craned his neck to see what I was doing. His eyes widened.

I tried the new numbers.

"6-11-1?" I said as I turned the dial.

The locker popped open. Juan Carlos grinned, but he still looked miserable.

"Oh man . . ." he said. A blush crept over his cheeks. "I hope the rest of the day isn't like this."

"It's going to be fine!" I said. "Just relax. Take a few deep breaths. After this summer, you can handle anything."

I realized this wasn't just Juan Carlos's first day of sixth grade, it was his first day at a whole new school after moving to town over the summer. Kareem and I were the only people he knew.

"We have science block first thing after homeroom. What could be better than that?!"

He nodded, but he didn't look convinced. I gave his shoulder a light punch and then continued down the hall. I hadn't seen Kareem yet, but he usually slid into his seat just in time, even if it was the first day of school.

"19-9-47," I whispered to myself as I made my way down to where I knew my locker would be. A lot of things made me nervous, but not school. The world often didn't make sense, but school always did. I found my locker—number 39—and confidently spun the combo lock to open it.

Nothing happened.

When I yanked on the lock, there was no click. I tried again. And again. Nothing happened!

"19-9-47," I said, and tried again. Nothing.

"Here, let me help," said a voice. A pair of hands appeared in front of my face. They belonged to a girl I'd never seen before—a girl with deep brown skin and thick hair braided into a halo around the top of her head. "19-9-47, right?"

She twirled the lock expertly, so fast I was sure she'd pass up the numbers. She did what *seemed* like the exact same thing I did, except this time the lock made a satisfying click sound and popped open.

"Sometimes they're tricky," she said with a big smile. Then she turned away and went striding down the hall.

"Who was that?" Juan Carlos said, appearing a second later. I don't know if he saw her open my locker or just noticed her confident aura the way I had.

"I have no idea," I said. Then I muttered so only I could hear, "Somebody who thinks they're some kind of safecracker."

"I'm going to be late," Juan Carlos said, looking a little alarmed. Boy, school really made him anxious. "I'll see you in science block, okay?"

I nodded, trying to shake off my interaction with the mystery girl. And by the time science block arrived, I had. School always made me feel good. Everything made sense at school, and it seemed like my new teachers were the kind of adults who would take the time to explain things if they didn't make sense—even if the things that didn't make sense were sometimes rules. My hopes were high walking into science block. I'd been hearing about how cool Ms. Erivo was for years, and envied all the sixth graders who took her class.

As soon as I walked in, I saw Juan Carlos and Kareem already inside. But then I saw someone else.

The girl from the hallway. The new girl. She was sitting in the seat I absolutely would have chosen, next to Kareem. The seat on the other side of Juan Carlos was open, and it would be fine to sit there. But the one next to Kareem was closer to the window and I prefer natural light when I'm in class. The fluorescent bulbs in school give me a headache.

Why did she sit next to Kareem? She doesn't even know him!

The new girl was sitting there leafing through papers in her folder. Kareem gave me an undercover shrug. It's not like he could tell her to move.

I plopped down next to Juan Carlos just as Ms. Erivo closed the door to the classroom and walked to the front of the room.

"Welcome!" she said. "Guess what? You're in sixth grade! This is going to be the best year ever!"

She almost shouted it. We all jumped a little, but the smile on her face was so infectious that we laughed. I heard Kareem chuckle. From the other side of him, I heard a loud chortle from the girl who had opened my locker for me. *Not for me*, I thought sourly. *Without asking. It's not like I needed her help.*

I had to pay attention now, because Ms. Erivo talked fast—so fast that she even taught us a hand signal that we could use if we ever needed her to slow down.

"Sometimes I get excited about science," she admitted, smiling. "And I'll do my best to slow down when you need me to. But consider this your heads-up: Things move fast in this classroom! Buckle up, Reese Cups!"

Ms. Erivo was the kind of teacher who made everything fun, even taking roll. She had us go around and introduce ourselves and share a fun fact. Some people were goofy.

"I sunburned my butt this summer," said Randy Pryce. Some teachers would shush the laughter, but Ms. Erivo cracked up right along with everyone else.

I knew I was going to talk about the Create Space for my fun fact. I wanted Ms. Erivo to know how serious I was about science. When it got to our row, the new girl went first. She even stood up.

"Hi, everyone. My name is Fatima Adebayo," she said, with the same confident tone that she had used in the hallway. "And a fun fact about me is that I'm an inventor. My favorite subset of physics is electromagnetism and I love trying to apply it into the real world. My parents helped me get patents on two of my inventions this summer. It's been an exciting time."

As Kareem started to go next, my mind drifted. *It's been an exciting time?* I said in my head. She talked like she thought she was a teacher, too; like she and Ms. Erivo were buddies! And patents? The purpose of fun facts wasn't to brag. I could feel myself scowling. Suddenly everything I had planned to say for my fun fact seemed ridiculous. I didn't even hear Juan Carlos's fact; my mind was racing, trying to find something I could say to one-up Fatima. I thought of Cheese. I guarantee Miss Two Patents had never met an alien life-form and helped it escape intergalactic hunters! But I couldn't say that. No one would believe me anyway.

Juan Carlos nudged me and I snapped out of it. Ms. Erivo was looking at me curiously, then glancing down at her clipboard of names. Who knows how long I'd been sitting there spaced out.

"Ethan Fairmont," I said quickly. "My name is Ethan Fairmont. And, uh, I'm an inventor too. I mean, I'm an inventor."

I slapped my forehead inwardly. *Too?!* That implied Fatima was an inventor first, and she definitely wasn't. And why didn't I say anything else? I wanted to add something, but Ms. Erivo had already moved on to the next person and I just felt silly. I glanced over at Fatima. She didn't seem to notice my blunder.

"Now," Ms. Erivo said when everyone had been introduced. "You have probably heard that I have a reputation for class projects. I love projects." I felt my heart start to lift again. I loved projects, too. "And this is going to be the biggest project you've had in your school career. You and your group will work together all semester long on a topic of your choosing. Now, I don't want us all to get up and move around, so I'm going to group you into threes by the desks you chose."

She walked to the back of the room, counting us off into threes. By the time she got to the front of the room, Juan Carlos was grinning and so was Kareem and so, of course, was I. We were going to get to work on the same project together all semester long!

"Ah, we have an odd number," Ms. Erivo said. I was too busy smiling at my friends to hear right away. "Fatima, you can join this group. We'll have one group of four. Now, let me tell you more about what I'll expect this semester . . ."

She went on talking but my smile was fading and I definitely wasn't listening anymore. I looked at Fatima and found her smirking in our direction. *She* had to be in *our* group? All semester long? What would have been the perfect project was absolutely ruined.

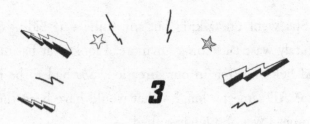

3

A SECRET GIFT

"Ethan, it can't be *that* bad," my dad said when I got home. He leaned on the counter and chomped on cucumbers with my brothers while I ranted about the new girl.

"It *is*, Dad," I raged. "She is the *worst*. She's a know-it-all and a bragger. Oh! You know what she did? She corrected Ms. Erivo! Ms. Erivo said it was 11:45 and Fatima said, 'Actually it's only 11:30.'"

"Sounds like someone else I know," Troy said, giving me a pointed look.

I glared at him.

"She thinks she's smarter than everyone," I growl. "She thinks she's some genius because she can open a locker."

"Uh, okay," Troy said. "That's specific."

"And I have to be around her all . . . semester . . . long," I went on. "She makes me nauseous."

"It sounds like you have a crush on her," my other brother Chris teased.

"No, no," our dad said, straightening up. "We don't speak like that about people. Especially not ones we have a crush on. Look, son," my dad continued, eating his last cucumber. "It sounds like Fatima hasn't done anything but make you feel a little insecure. Deal with that on your own time but don't you even think about going to school and making the new kid feel uncomfortable. Focus that energy on coming up with a great idea for your semester project, got it?"

"Yes," I said glumly, and what I didn't say out loud was that I didn't think there was anything that could make Fatima Adebaya feel uncomfortable.

I picked at my after-school snack, still feeling low. The first day of school is usually the best day ever, but today felt off. Maybe it was because I was still thinking about Cheese.

The sound of my mom getting home from work made us all lift our heads. Dad was always happy when she got home, but today his smile was extra big. When she came into the kitchen, she and Dad made eye contact. They were doing that thing where parents are talking right in front of you without saying a word. She raised an eyebrow, and he pursed his lips with a half-hidden smile.

"Hi, Mom," I said suspiciously. She hadn't even said hello to me yet!

"Hello, Ethan," she said. "I'm glad you're here. Your father and I have something we want to talk to you about."

If it wasn't for their smiles, I would feel anxious thinking they knew something about Cheese—even though there was nothing to know now that Cheese was gone. But still, they're acting weird. I'm afraid they're going to tell me something they thought was exciting but wasn't, like a family trip to a cabin with no WiFi. But it was the first day of school. There was no way we were going on vacation any time soon.

"Yeah?" I said slowly.

They exchanged another look, smiling. Then my mom reached into her purse. She pulled something out, placed it on the counter, and scooted it across to me.

"Well, you're getting older. And you proved to be so responsible over the summer, helping Mrs. McGee and all."

Boy, if they only knew what I was really doing over the summer.

"So, your father and I have decided to get you a cell phone!"

I think I'm hearing things. I remembered very clearly asking them for a phone like a billion times last year and being told no a billion times in return. But now here they were smiling at me and sitting on the counter between us was a new cell phone.

"Is this a trick?" I said, not yet daring to reach for the phone. "Are you pranking me?"

"No, Ethan," my dad said. "We've been talking about it for a while now, and we think you've shown a lot of maturity with the Create Space. And after everything that happened in the neighborhood this summer, we want to make sure you have what you need to be safe and to be able to call us if you need us."

Using his index finger, my dad inched the phone toward me.

I slowly reached for the brand-new phone, picking it up and examining it.

"We know it isn't the most advanced thing in the world, but it's something," my mom said.

"No, it's perfect," I said. And I meant it. Having a phone at all was amazing. Besides, I could always try my own special upgrades if I ever got the itch.

"There's one condition," my mom said. Her eyebrows arched.

"Okay . . ."

"You can't turn this into one of your experiments."

"Huh?"

"Ethan, you have turned everything from blenders to calculators into random inventions." My dad laughed. "And we love your curious spirit. But you absolutely, positively, 100 percent cannot turn this phone into something else. I don't care if it's an invention that would carry our house to the Moon, you understand?"

They're joking, but they're also dead serious. I quickly swallowed and gave them my most trustworthy face.

"I definitely understand," I said. "Thank you."

They gave me a mini-lecture on parental controls and all that stuff, which I've heard my friends talk about from their parents. No big deal. I just wanted to get up to my room and do stuff with it. With *my phone*. They've already put their contacts plus the numbers for Juan Carlos and Kareem in there. Wow.

I felt like a balloon. The helium from getting my own phone carried me all the way upstairs to my room. When I got there, I stood in the middle of the room, staring down at the phone in my hands. My own phone! I could call *my* friends on *my* phone.

Well, not all my friends.

As excited as I was, my heart sank a little. Once again, I was thinking of Cheese. Where was the alien now? What amazing things was it seeing? Was Cheese thinking of me and Juan Carlos and Kareem? Was Cheese safe? Even with the shiny new phone in my palm, I couldn't help but feel a little let down. When I was little and missing my grandpa in Georgia, my mom would tell me to look at the Moon, because no matter where I was, Grandpa was seeing the same Moon. But that couldn't be true for Cheese. Out there in deep space, there were millions of moons.

Still looking at my phone, I took a step and tripped over an old xylophone I was trying to turn into a musical calculator. I decided to go with it, and continued my journey down to the floor, resting my back against my bed. I held my new phone up in front of my face.

There was something about having a phone that made me feel more like an adult. Even though I shouldn't care, I wondered if Fatima had one.

"She has two patents," I grumbled to myself. "Of course she has a phone. Probably invented her own."

I played with the settings on my phone, wanting to explore it a bit before texting my friends. I changed the brightness, changed the ringtone. What else? I opened the Bluetooth menu. I remember a while back I borrowed Chris's Bluetooth speaker, fully intending to give it back, but it got lost in the mess of inventions in my room. I scanned the disaster of my bedroom. Maybe if I connected it to my phone, I could ping it and find the speaker.

I turned the Bluetooth on my phone on and waited. Sure enough, a second later, I heard a soft *chirp*. It was coming from behind me. Under the bed! Way in the back, I could see something glowing under my bed. I grinned. My brother was so annoyed when I lost the speaker, but now I could say I knew where it was all along.

The glow under my bed came from the back, almost against the wall. I stretched as much as I could but couldn't reach the speaker. So I went into the laundry room just outside my door and grabbed a broom.

When I returned to my room, I used the broom like an extended arm. I hooked the speaker and brought it out into the light. I saw right away that it wasn't my brother's speaker. But I did recognize it.

It was a light-flower, powering a mysterious device.

It didn't look like the light-flowers I'd seen on Cheese's ship, though. Its stem was gold and the petals were purple. And the light inside the flower was a faint blue, which is probably why I didn't notice it before.

Any sinking my heart had done now buoyed up to Mt. Everest levels. Cheese left me something! I was as sure of it as I was that the sky was blue. Cheese had left me this on purpose. But what was "this"? Now that it was in my hands, I could see the attached device more clearly. It was a slim, shiny object that was warm to the touch and vibrated silently under my fingertips.

I felt like I was vibrating, too. Excitement and hope were fizzing inside me like I was a shaken can of Coke. I wanted to text Kareem and Juan Carlos immediately, but I knew there would be a bunch of questions that I couldn't answer yet.

I needed to run more tests.

4

EAVESDROPPING

Beside me, Nugget sat on the bed nibbling a guinea pig snack and watching me fiddle with the light-flower device Cheese had hidden under my bed. It had been hours and I was no closer to figuring out what it did.

"What do you think, Nugget?" I muttered, holding the device up to the light. "What would Cheese have left me? Something that can help with my inventions? Maybe a power source . . . ?"

"Maybe it communicates with Cheese's ship," I mused. "Like a homing beacon."

I thought about all the brain-busting we did to figure out how to make the light-flowers grow and get Cheese's ship back into space. Sometimes things aren't as complicated as they seem. Sometimes they are simple. Right in front of your face.

I glanced down at my shiny new phone, sitting on the bed just far enough from Nugget that he wouldn't get any ideas about nibbling it, but something was off. I realized that my Bluetooth was connected to a device—but I hadn't set anything up yet. I felt my eyes widen.

"Of course!" I cried. Nugget squeaked, dropping his snack in surprise.

I cut off my phone and stared at Cheese's device in my hand. The faint light inside faded away. I turned my phone back on and, sure enough, the device gave a light chirp and the light-flower began to glow.

"Whoaaa . . ."

It was responding to my cell phone.

"I think it's a communication device! Cheese wants to talk as much as I do! I just need to figure out how to make it work."

I believed that I could. Dad was always saying that the real key to success was tenacity, no matter what you were trying to accomplish. And if there was any project that I was going to be tenacious about, it was this one. The hardest part was already done for me. The invention existed! I just had to figure out how to make it work.

No way Fatima Adebayo could do something like this.

I thought about the group project for Ms. Erivo's class. What if we found a way to communicate with Cheese and our project was all about deep-space inter-action? That would be cool *and* guarantee that Ms. Erivo saw that I was just as good an inventor as Fatima—no, better.

I fiddled around with my phone while I plotted. I set up the facial recognition feature, turning my face this way and that to lock in my image. Next up: tinkering with Cheese's phone, or whatever it was, to try to activate it. But, first, I needed a snack.

Nugget was always munching on something, and even though he was a guinea pig, his appetite was infectious. I carefully stowed Cheese's device back under the bed, then I headed to the kitchen.

The house was dark and quiet, perfect for a late-night snack. I hadn't noticed it had gotten so late. At this hour, no one would ask me what I was working on or follow me up to my room.

I dug around in the refrigerator, thinking about all the foods Cheese loved to eat. The very first day we met, we thought Cheese was going to eat *us*! It's easy to be afraid of something you don't understand. I see why people get weird about aliens. But Cheese was a living creature who came in peace. It was simple.

I loaded up a plate with cold pickles and sandwich meat. Nothing from bags that would crinkle like an alarm system. I balanced the plate on one hand, using my other hand to keep the pile of snacks from wobbling. Now the tricky part: getting past Mom and Dad's door. It's always when you think you're close to success that disaster can jump up and bite you.

I stepped carefully, avoiding known squeaky spots, doing my best to stay silent. But when I got close to my parents' door, I realized that I didn't have to worry about waking them up—they were already awake. Mom had switched out of the night shift a few weeks ago and I was still getting used to her being here at night. I paused. I could hear them talking, and in kind of raised voices.

"Mrs. McGee got three times what she paid," Dad was saying. "That's significant."

"It is," my mother agreed. "It definitely is. I just don't know. It seems too good to be true."

I knew I wasn't supposed to eavesdrop, but something in my parents' voices made my sneaking feet stop and my ears sharpen to listen.

"In a way it is," my father said. "Boomx Industries, that big tech chain, is setting up shop five miles from here. Everyone they hired is moving here from places like New York and Los Angeles. They have money to burn. If we found the right buyer, we could stand to make a lot of money."

"Yes," my mother said reluctantly. "But selling the house—"

"I know," my father agreed, sounding sad. "I know. But college for the boys is getting expensive. And we still have Ethan to put through."

"Yes, but he'll get scholarships," Mom said. I couldn't see her face on the other side of the door, but I could picture her expression just by hearing her voice: pinched with worry, but thinking hard. Mom was always trying to consider all the angles and do the right thing.

"I know he's a genius, but it feels wrong to just assume that and not be prepared. And selling the house for the kind of money Mrs. McGee got for hers would certainly help a lot. Just something to consider," Dad said. "We don't have to decide right now. Let's think about it. Come on, it's late."

Their voices got softer then, too soft for me to hear. I looked down at the plate full of snacks in my hand. My appetite was gone. I stood there in the dark of the house, wishing I could knock on my parents' door and assure them I'll be fine. I wish I could go in and ask them the million questions zipping around in my mind.

Are you really going to sell our house?

Are we running out of money?

Where is Mrs. McGee going to live?

Is everything going to be okay?

But I didn't knock on their door, and I didn't go wake up my brothers, either, even though I really wanted to. Instead,

I carried my snack upstairs, set the plate on the dresser, and flopped onto my bed. I had a phone to text my friends if I wanted to, to tell them everything.

But I didn't. What I would say? Some things are too sad for words. Sometimes all you can be is silent.

JODIE

"Have y'all noticed that there are a lot more people coming here than there used to be?" Kareem said as we locked up the Create Space. It was later than when we typically left, mostly because there were so many people finishing projects and hanging out and talking.

"It's been getting more and more popular," said Juan Carlos. "I thought maybe people would just come to the opening day and then disappear, but nope. They keep coming back. And more and more."

"Yeah," Kareem said. "But I don't just mean here. I mean Ferrous City in general. Like, there's more traffic, there are more people walking around. The bakery has been selling out every day! It used to be I could get there at 7:45 in the morning and still get a doughnut but now if I'm not there by 7, forget about it!"

I nodded as the three of us made our way down the sidewalk, thinking of what I'd heard my parents discussing.

"Yeah, there's a big tech company opening up," I said. "So, all these tech people are coming to work there."

"Even I noticed lots of new shops popping up," Juan Carlos said. "One after another."

"I guess it's a good thing," Kareem said. "More options and stuff. I'm kind of mad about the doughnuts, though."

I wanted to say something about what I'd heard Mom and Dad talking about last night. How this felt related— people buying the houses and selling them for more because of some new company. All of a sudden, people thought this was a good place to live. But it always had been. To me, any-way. It was the same old place with the same old corners and the same neighbors I'd known my whole life. Well, except Mrs. McGee, now that she was moving. My heart squeezed a little bit. Who else would leave? Maybe it wouldn't matter. If *we* left, I wouldn't even know what changed and what stayed the same.

"Hey, what's wrong?" Kareem asked, nudging me as we turned a corner. "You have your gloomy face on."

"I don't have a gloomy face," I said, rolling my eyes. I'd never felt gloomy until lately. Things felt different. Life was changing. Inside me and outside me. "I'm fine."

"Not for long," Juan Carlos said. "Brace yourselves."

I looked up from where I'd been staring at my feet, just in time to see two people crossing the street straight toward us.

"Is that—" I started.

"Jodie," Kareem groaned.

"Hey!" Jodie called. He had a big personality. I hadn't seen him the whole first week of school, and it was out of sight, out of mind. Now he was right in front of me and there was no escape. "Have you thought any more about joining AHA? Mr. Jensen at school said we can use his classroom in the afternoons to hold meetings."

"Um—" I started, but he interrupted me.

"What's to think about?" he said in his loud voice. "Aren't you curious about everything that's happening all over the country?"

"Um, *what's* happening all over the country?" Juan Carlos asked.

"Alien appearances, of course," Jodie said. Kareem being Kareem, kept moving down the sidewalk instead of pausing to talk to him, but Jodie didn't seem to notice. He fell in step beside us, talking a mile a minute. "People in small towns all across the country have been observing what could be alien contact. Town after town after town! And Ferrous City is no different! I've been keeping careful tabs on the chatter in Ferrous City—"

"The *chatter*?" Kareem questioned.

"Yes, the conversations people are having online and in the news about occurrences they've witnessed," Jodie said patiently. "And Ferrous City has had an uptick in unusual observations. I don't know what you guys were up to this summer, but—"

"Nothing at all," Juan Carlos said quickly, and kind of loudly. Not cool. "Just normal summer stuff. Completely normal."

Kareem elbowed him before I could.

Jodie chattered on. "There were a couple weird people roaming Ferrous City that my brother and I personally believe to be special agents from the FBI or some organization that tracks alien activity. Have you ever seen *Men in Black*? I'm not saying it's *just* like *Men in Black*, but—"

"What does AHA stand for again?" Kareem interrupted.

"Aliens Have Arrived!" Jodie announced in a theatrical voice. "You really should join the group. Maybe we can all meet at the Create Space soon?

Jodie went on and on. There was no way to interrupt him that didn't feel suspicious. Every time Juan Carlos looked like he was going to speak I shot him a look that told him to zip it. He was sweating and he wasn't the most reliable when he was nervous. Honestly, I didn't feel reliable, either. We thought we were done with being questioned and followed now that the Others were gone, but here we were again.

Cheese wasn't here, so it's not like they could find our alien friend. But what if there was evidence we had overlooked, or evidence we didn't even know was evidence? Jodie might be kind of annoying, but he was committed. He probably knew what to look for. And maybe if I hadn't had my experience with Cheese, Jodie wouldn't come off as so annoying. Who knows, maybe we could've been friends. But with me being worried about Cheese, and Jodie so dedicated to finding out the truth, he was a pain in my side.

"What do you think?" Jodie said, clearly talking to me.

"Uh, I gotta ask my mom," I said. Kareem shot me a disgusted look. *What?* I mouthed. Unlike Kareem, I didn't care about looking cool, and moms were the best excuses for everything. Don't want to hang out? My mom said I can't. Don't want to have somebody over? My mom said no company. Easy.

"No biggie," Jodie said easily. "Talk to her and let us know. AHA is actively recruiting because we know these appearances aren't going to stop. There's momentum now, and AHA won't rest until we know why! We'll scour this whole town if we have to."

I tried to laugh in a way that didn't sound nervous. Why did everyone have to be so nosy?! I thought of Cheese's phone hidden under my bed in my room. It's not like Jodie could get into my room without my permission, but, still, Cheese had left me the device so we could communicate with each other. But what if it ended up getting used as evidence? It made me want to leave the phone under my bed and never try to reach Cheese at all. Maybe that's the best way to keep Cheese safe, by forgetting about aliens entirely.

Jodie split off when we got closer to the park.

"Too many people," Jodie said, waving. "No way aliens would show up here. I like to stay to quieter parts of Ferrous City where there's a greater chance of an AHA moment."

"Uh, sure," Kareem said. "See ya."

We watched Jodie go. When he was completely out of sight, I breathed a sigh of relief.

6

THE COURTS

RJ had just finished a game of pickup when we arrived at the picnic tables outside the courts at Hathaway Park. He was sweating something serious and still catching his breath. I glanced at Kareem, wondering if he wanted to play, but while he gave a head nod to some of the guys on the court, he didn't make a move. He hadn't been as interested in sports lately. He never said anything about it, and I didn't know how to ask. You would think that after his summer we could talk about anything, but some things are tricky no matter what.

"Who was that dude y'all were walking with?" RJ asked as he cooled off, stretching while holding onto the chain-link fence.

"Jodie," I said. "You know him?"

"Nah, not really."

"He's into aliens," Kareem said, in a low voice.

RJ raised his eyebrows. "You mean . . . ?"

"He doesn't know anything about Cheese," I said quickly. "I mean, not really. He definitely doesn't know we were involved. But he's asking questions."

"Man, I thought we were done with all that," RJ groaned. He stopped stretching and flung himself onto the bench of the picnic table.

"Me, too, trust me," I said. But that wasn't entirely true. Everyone else considered Cheese a closed chapter. The alien was gone, that was it, *the end*. But it never felt like the end to me. Especially not now that I had discovered what I thought was a communication device Cheese had left me in my room.

"How do you know he doesn't know anything?" RJ said.

"He was asking a bunch of questions," Juan Carlos said. "He wants to, like, recruit us."

"Might make sense to join," RJ said, shrugging.

"*What?*" I cried.

"Excuse me?" Kareem said, looking outraged.

"Hear me out," RJ said. "If you join this little group, then at least you'll know what he's up to. You can even, like, give him false leads, you know?"

"What does that mean?" Juan Carlos said.

"You know, like in some detective shows, the killer or whoever will drop clues but they actually lead in the wrong direction. It's a diversion. You could do that with the alien kid."

"You mean infiltrate," I said.

"Yep, that's exactly what I mean. Shoot, maybe I'll do it. Sounds fun."

I considered RJ's idea. It might work. But it also felt a lot like blatantly lying, and I wasn't good at that. There had to be a better—and easier—way to protect Cheese.

"I think he'll go away on his own," Kareem said. "He's obsessed for now but once school gets going and he realizes that nobody wants to be in his weird little group, it'll fade away. I don't think we need to worry about it."

"I hope not," Juan Carlos said, looking worried.

"Heads-up," somebody on the court called. "Twelve."

We froze. RJ stopped rubbing his neck. Juan Carlos stopped fiddling with an acorn on the table. Kareem stopped rolling RJ's ball between his hands. I stopped scratching the bug bite on my arm. We sat motionless as a police car rolled down the street next to the park. It seemed to move in slow motion, the two White uniformed men inside staring out their windows at us and at the guys on the basketball court.

"What are they looking at?" RJ muttered.

I was glad he didn't say it any louder. I already felt like my heartbeat was as loud as a cannon. My chest was so tight I thought my lungs might pop under the pressure. I will go days without thinking about it, but then on days like today, the police rolling past and the air quiet, it all comes plunging back into my head. The day the cops came to our house and put Dad in cuffs. It felt so far away but also so close that it was breathing down my neck.

"We're not doing anything wrong," Juan Carlos said under his breath, but we all knew it didn't matter. My dad hadn't been doing anything wrong, either. We all shared the memory of what happened that day, and I knew the other guys had their own memories, too. Days where, instead of cruising by, the car found a reason to stop.

Today, though, they kept going. This whole side of the park stayed silent for a moment more until somebody tossed a joke on the court and everybody exploded into laughter. I felt myself relaxing. No matter how tense things got, there was always the moment after the tension when we all returned to the thing that brought us to the park to begin with. We were all bonded more than we knew.

"I need to tell you something," I said. "I found something in my room last night."

"A squirrel's nest?" Kareem teased. "With all that mess in there, I wouldn't be surprised."

"Excuse me?!" I cried. "For your information, I actually cleaned my room last night."

"I'd have to see it to believe it," Juan Carlos said. "Hard evidence."

"I took a picture," I said proudly, pulling out my phone and searching for the picture. I did it all nonchalant, but I wanted my friends to notice.

"Since when do you have your own phone?" RJ said.

"Since yesterday," I grinned.

"It's about time!" he said.

"Yeah, yeah," I said sliding over my phone. "Anyway, here's what I found in my room. Check it out. I think it's a phone."

"Wait," Juan Carlos said, looking confused. "You have *two* phones?"

"Yes. Well, no. I mean, kind of."

"Is it an old iPhone you're trying to fix or something?" Kareem said.

"No—" I started.

"How do you forget you have two phones?" RJ asked.

"I didn't! Geez, look at the picture! I think it's an *alien* phone," I shouted to shut them up. Then I clapped my hand over my mouth and gazed frantically around the park to make sure Jodie hadn't changed his mind and hung around. I dropped my voice to a whisper. "Cheese left it for me."

"*What?* When?" Kareem whispered back.

"I don't know," I went on. "I found it hidden under my bed. From what I can tell, it's powered by Bluetooth, or UHFs."

"UHFs?" Juan Carlos asked.

"Yeah, ultra-high radio frequencies, it's a type of electromagnetic wave. Anyway, I'm pretty sure it's a communication device, I just have to figure out how to use it."

"Oh, no," Juan Carlos said, not looking excited. "Don't let Jodie in your house. Ever."

"Trust me, I'm already thinking about it," I answered.

"So you haven't used it yet?" RJ said.

"No, but once I figure out how it works, I will," I said. I cast a glance at Kareem and Juan Carlos. "I was kind of thinking we could make it our semester-long project for science block. Like, not the phone itself, because that has to stay a secret, obviously. But maybe we can do something about deep-space communication! Then we can work on contacting Cheese at the same time."

Kareem's eyes lit up. He hated projects, so any idea that he didn't have to come up with was a good one. Juan Carlos, on the other hand, looked less enthusiastic.

"What about Fatima?" he said. "Do you think she'll want to?"

I gritted my teeth. How did I forget about Fatima again?

"She'll come around," I said. "I'll convince her. Won't be a problem at all."

GROUP LEADER

Surprise: It was a problem.

When I sat down in science block, I had a whole plan of what I was going to say to pitch my idea of making a communication device for our semester-long project. Last week, Ms. Erivo told us that we should be thinking about a list of things we could possibly work on as a group that we could all agree on, and I had thought of nothing else. I didn't exactly have a list of possible projects, but I definitely had a list of reasons why we should study deep-space communication. Mainly: Cheese. But obviously Fatima couldn't know that, so I had to be careful in how I pitched the idea.

"You really think she's going to go for it?" Kareem said quietly next to me. Class still had five minutes before it started and Fatima hadn't arrived yet. Kareem, Juan Carlos, and I were huddled together in Ms. Erivo's room discussing the plan.

"I mean, she won't really have a choice," I said. "There are four of us in the group and three of us want to do deep-space communication. If she doesn't agree with all my arguments, then we'll just take a vote. We outnumber her."

"That would make me mad if I was her," Juan Carlos said, shrugging.

"I don't care if she's mad," I said sourly.

Kareem gave me a look that kind of reminded me of my dad.

"Okay, it's not that I don't *care*," I said. "It's just that this is important. And we can't let her stand in the way of something of this magnitude."

"Of what magnitude?" Fatima said, appearing next to Juan Carlos. We all jumped.

"Um, nothing," I said as she took her seat. She shrugged and went to unpack her stuff for class. I glanced at her notebook and had to look away. *How was her handwriting so perfect?* It was like a computer had typed it. Not loopy and pretty, just neat and organized. Bulleted lists and stuff. *What wasn't she good at?*

"Okay," Ms. Erivo said after starting class and taking roll. "I'm going to let you discuss with your groups before we get started. These projects aren't the *only* thing we'll be working on this year, but they are a big part of this semester, so I want to give you plenty of time to decide what you'll be doing."

I turned to Fatima, taking a deep breath as I prepared to rattle off my script of why we should do a communication device. But Fatima was already turning to us.

"Okay," she said in a calm voice. "I took the weekend to think about the list of ideas Ms. Erivo asked us to prepare, and I think I have some good options. I figured that we're going to be learning all kinds of different science this year, so we should pick something that can have different types of science apply to it. Something along the lines of climate or city planning."

I stared at her, my head swirling. How could any one person be this annoying? Who put her in charge of this operation? Who did she think she was, thinking she could steer the whole project?

"We want to do a study of deep-space communication," I interrupted. I didn't even look at Kareem or Juan Carlos to see what their reactions were. "There's, um, a ton of new research that digs into the possibilities that are out there."

She stopped abruptly, surprised by the fact that I interrupted her. Or maybe surprised by my tone. The way she squinted kind of looked like she was annoyed.

"Okay," she said slowly, looking between each of our faces. "Why?"

"Why deep space?" I snapped. "Do you ever need a why for deep space? It's deep space!"

She blinked patiently, and that made me feel even madder.

"Okay, why communication?"

"Because that's what we want to do," I said. "And because communication is important. And, uh, the future of our planet could change a lot based on what's, um, out there."

To my surprise, she nodded.

"That makes sense," she said. "And technology is one of the things on my list that could have multiple kinds of science applied to it. It's always changing, and that's good to study, too."

"Yeah," I said weakly. I had been so surprised by her taking charge of the conversation that I forgot my whole script of why we should do deep-space communication. But she seemed to already be making her own script.

"It could work," she said. "We'd have to consider a power source, which is always a big part of science. I'm sure Ms. Erivo will be talking to us about circuits and electricity and stuff, so we can build that in."

She mused out loud for another minute, as if convincing herself that it was a workable plan. I looked at Kareem and Juan Carlos, who had both been sitting silently, like they were watching a battle at the Coliseum.

"After all," she said. "Did you hear about NASA's Deep Space station? It's called Deep Space Station 53. It's in Madrid. We have a lot of research to lean on. So okay, I'm fine with this. I guess the only thing to do is to decide on a group leader."

She smiled brightly. I already knew she was going to say she should be the leader. It made my throat tighten up. Who did she think she was?

"I think it should be Juan Carlos," she said.

I felt my eyes bug out.

"What?" Juan Carlos said.

"Yeah," she said, shrugging. "You don't talk much. I think if you're the leader, it might help you be more involved."

Before I could open my mouth to argue, Juan Carlos said, "Okay."

I looked at him in shock, but he was looking at Fatima. I would be a real jerk for arguing now, and, whatever, she agreed to do deep-space communication, and I thought that would be a huge fight. I clamped my mouth shut.

"Everyone decided?" Ms. Erivo called over the buzz of conversation a few minutes later. "Good. Let's set the projects aside for the rest of class and move into the lesson I have planned."

Fatima had a special folder just for projects. I glared at her as she closed it and pulled out another folder. On the front she had written in her computer handwriting: *General*

Science. It made me want to label all my folders, too, to be super organized so she didn't think she was the only one who could do stuff like that. In the end I just rolled my eyes and turned to Ms. Erivo.

○

"She's not so bad," Juan Carlos said when we all walked into the lunchroom later. "She's brainy. My prima is like that. Sometimes brainy people act different. It's okay."

I scowled as we crossed toward the lunch line. I wanted to say *You're only saying that because she said you should be the leader* but I didn't want to be mean, so I just let it go. Maybe I was just hungry and that's why I was feeling so irritable.

"She could be cool," Kareem said. "She's just kinda bossy. But my dad says to be friends with bossy girls because when they grow up they'll probably be president or senator or something."

The idea of Fatima being president made me want to flee the country.

"What is that?" Juan Carlos said when we got up to the lunch counter.

"Meat loaf, sweetie," the lunch lady said as she handed us trays.

"Luckily, I have a backup lunch," I muttered. The meat loaf looked like it should be someone's semester-long science project.

I waited while Kareem and Juan Carlos got their trays and then we all trooped over to the tables. I got the feeling that someone was staring at me. I swiveled my head to look for who it might be. My eyes landed on two faces I recognized. The first was Jodie, the AHA kid, sitting at a table alone. He was staring intently at me and Kareem and Juan Carlos. I didn't really like the expression on his face, like he was studying me for information. I turned away and scanned the cafeteria. "There's Di," I said, pointing at RJ's sister. "Let's go sit with her."

I hadn't seen Di much since the summer. She was always busy with tons of clubs and teams. Captain of the Basketball Team, president of the Nature Club, all that stuff. Today she was leaning over a notebook, but she looked up when we all sat down.

"Hey y'all," she said. "You remembered to sign up for the recycling drive, right?"

"Yeah," Kareem said. "I got a dude in my Language Arts class to sign up, too."

"Thanks!" she beamed.

"Why aren't you eating?" I said. She had no tray, no lunch bag, just the notebook.

Her big smile faded. It made me feel worried for some reason, seeing her look sad.

"I don't eat meat," she said. "And the only thing they're serving is meat loaf."

"I would give you my mashed potatoes," Juan Carlos said as we slid onto an empty bench in the lunchroom, "but I already ate them."

We all stopped as our heads turns to Juan's plate. He wasn't lying, the mashed potatoes had vanished.

"Jeez, not even I eat that fast," shouted Kareem. "We just sat down."

"The mashed potatoes are my favorite thing here!"

"Here, have some of my sandwich," I said quickly before the shouting match began. "It's peanut butter and jelly. No meat."

Her frown brightened a little bit, and it put me in a better mood.

"Are you sure, Ethan?"

"Yeah, of course," I said, reaching into the bag and pulling out the other half that I hadn't bitten yet. "I can't just let you be hungry!"

She reached out for the sandwich, smiling, and when she took it from my hand, our fingers brushed against each other. My stomach felt like it was a balloon being twisted into the shape of a circus animal. When Di said *Thank you*, I could barely make myself say *You're welcome*. Where did this nervousness come from?! And why? I'd known Di and her brother forever.

To distract myself, I opened up my bag of Doritos and plopped them between us.

"There," I said, "now you won't be hungry."

"Thanks, Ethan," she said again.

"What are friends for?" I gulped.

CRUSH? NO WAY.

Juan Carlos and Kareem both got rides home from school. I made my way back to my house alone. Today I didn't mind. I needed to think, and even though I usually did my best thinking with Nugget sitting on my lap, while I was petting his soft back, today I just stared at my feet as I slowly made my way home.

What was my problem?!

The shaken-up-Coke-bottle feeling just wouldn't go away. I missed Cheese. I didn't like Fatima. I felt weird about Di. I kept thinking about what I had overheard my parents saying about selling our house, and I had no one to talk to about it. I wished more than ever that I could contact Cheese. I didn't necessarily think that the alien would understand, either, just because everything was so complicated.

But I somehow felt that seeing Cheese would make things make sense. Maybe it would remind me of something important, something that could tie all this together.

I was more determined than ever to get straight to work figuring out the communication device.

But first, as usual, food.

I tossed my backpack on the couch and trooped into the kitchen. I found my dad already there, washing his hands. He was wearing grass-stained pants and a dirt-covered shirt. I knew he'd been weeding the garden. That's what Dad did to help clear his head when things felt messy. I wondered if he was thinking about selling the house while he pulled weeds, if he was trying to make things make sense, too. I wanted to ask, but I also didn't want to admit that I'd been eavesdropping. And maybe I was also a little nervous about what he'd say if I asked. Did I really want to know the truth?

"Hey, Ethan," he said, looking up from his soapy hands. "How was your day?"

"Fine," I said. "Do we have deli meat? I'm starving."

He glanced at my empty lunch bag.

"Maybe I need to start packing you a bigger lunch if you're so starving," he said. "You're getting older and might need—"

"No, it's not that," I said shaking my head. "I shared my lunch with Di."

"Di? Diamond?"

"Yeah, she didn't have a backup lunch on meat-loaf day. She's a vegetarian."

"It was nice of you to share your food with her," he said.

Thoughts of the house being sold melted away and were replaced with thoughts of Di. I remembered how it felt when our fingers brushed against each other as I passed her the sandwich. I felt my cheeks blaze with a blush.

"I mean, she's my friend," I said. "I couldn't just let her be hungry. Meat loaf is gross. And they should really offer more vegetarian options."

My dad moved to dry his hands while I made myself a snack. He nodded as I talked, saying nothing. This was one thing I liked about talking to my dad. It was like talking to yourself, and you could just let your thoughts come out.

"It's pretty cool that Di is a vegetarian," I said. "Like, she just decided to be. I remember last year people made fun of her because she just one day stopped eating chicken and stuff. But she didn't care at all."

"She sounds cool," my dad said.

"She is now," I said, thinking about the way I thought about her last summer, before everything with Cheese. I couldn't tell him all that, so I kept my response vague. "I mean, I didn't used to think so. But I guess maybe she's different now. She's really . . . nice. To lots of people. I didn't used to think she was nice, but she is."

"People change," my dad said. I could hear the smile in his voice.

"Yeah. I think she's really cool," I said. It felt like a decision—like something that was uncertain felt certain. "She *is* really cool."

"She sounds *amazing*," Troy said, appearing in the kitchen. He had a big smile on his face that I could tell had a joke attached to it. "I have a feeling you will advocate for vegetarian food fearlessly on her behalf."

"What do you mean?" I asked. "It's not just about Di. Lots of people are vegetarian. It doesn't make sense that if you're vegetarian your only option for lunch should be *mashed potatoes*."

"Is that what she was eating? Mashed potatoes?"

"No," I said. "I shared my sandwich with her."

"Did she ask you to?"

"No, I offered. Why? And why are you looking at me like that?!"

Troy glanced at my dad, who made an *I ain't in it* face, which was even more confusing. It was like there was a secret language being spoken right in front of me. But also, a part of me understood. And I knew it had to do with the way I felt when Di's fingers brushed mine.

"Maybe you should pack something special for tomorrow." Troy said, grinning. "Just for Di. You know, in case they're only serving chicken fingers."

I scowled at him because it was obvious that he was messing with me, but I also considered this. It would make her smile. And it felt really good when Di smiled.

"Like what?" I said, thinking out loud. "Maybe more chips or something."

"Aha!" Troy crowed. "I knew it! You have a crush!"

"I do not!" I cried. "She's my friend. It's not a big deal."

"Oh, yeah?"

"Yes," I snapped. "She's cool. Stop being weird!"

My dad passed me the bag of Cheetos that I couldn't reach on top of the fridge. I had to use every muscle in my body to keep from snatching it. It wasn't Dad's fault that Troy was so annoying.

"Don't you have somewhere to be?" I growled as I passed my brother on the way to my room. "Work or something *useful*?"

He called after me as I climbed the stairs, but I blocked it out and ignored him, the fiery feeling in my chest carrying me all the way to my room. Once up there, I forced myself not to slam the door, or my dad would walk all the way up here to lecture me about it. All the relief I felt from talking to Dad disappeared after the conversation with Troy—if you could call that a conversation. Why did people have to make everything complicated? Why did everything have to *be* complicated?

Things used to be so simple.

Nugget greeted me with a squeak. I let him out of his cage to explore the floor while I ate my sandwich. Dad made the best sandwiches and I *was* really hungry after only eating a half a lunch today. Maybe I would pack something for Di tomorrow. You know, just in case.

Nugget crawled under my bed, and it was like he was urging me to snap out of it and get focused on Cheese's communication device. I wolfed down the rest of my sandwich and crouched down to pull the glowing phone out.

I had to be able to figure this out! There had to be something simple that I needed to add or fix or adjust to make it work. It was alien technology, so I didn't expect it to be second nature, but also, I had helped Cheese with his ship and figured *that* out, so I knew I could do this, too. It would just take time.

My phone pinged with a text message. I jumped, forgetting I even had a phone. It was from Kareem, to both me and Juan Carlos:

I'm glad Fatima agreed to do the deep-space project. But how are we gonna keep her from finding out more than she needs to know? About you-know-who?

I hadn't thought about that problem. All I'd been thinking about was using as much time as possible to work on the project to find a way to talk to Cheese.

Good question, I said. Then I chose a thinking emoji.

My mom always says *We'll cross that bridge when we come to it*, so I typed that back, too. Honestly, I didn't even want to think about that bridge. I had too many other bridges in my way right now.

I carried Cheese's device over to my window to sit in the sunshine and study its mechanisms. My theory was still that the Bluetooth triggered something in Cheese's phone. That must be why Cheese couldn't turn on the device. In any case, now that it was on, I have to figure this thing out. On my phone, you tapped the person's name to call them. What was the Cheese version of that? I turned the device over and over in my hands. Everything was smooth. No buttons, no nothing. What was I supposed to press? I thought back to how Juan Carlos had drawn pictures to communicate with Cheese. I wish Cheese had left me a drawing of how to use this thing! What if I never figured it out? Being given the gift of an intergalactic phone and then never being able to use it because my brain was too tiny had to be the most frustrating hypothetical ever.

I rested my chin on my hand and stared out the window, looking for inspiration. Juan Carlos was right. There *were* more people in Ferrous City. This time last year, my street would usually be quiet. But people passed pretty regularly now, on their way to the shops or wherever. People change, my dad said. And so do places.

I kept watching. I was surprised when I recognized a familiar shape walking down the block. Jodie. He walked slowly, looking straight ahead. He didn't look in the direction of my house, but I got the feeling he was peeking from the corners of his eyes. I didn't know how he knew where I lived. It's not like he could have followed me home from school if he was just now passing by.

I watched him until he disappeared down the block, trying to fight the nervous feeling in my stomach.

ADULT LINGO IS THE WORST

Who needed an alarm clock when you had a manic guinea pig who ran in his wheel as soon as the sun rose? This time, though, instead of tossing a wadded-up candy wrapper at his cage and hissing at him to be quiet, I was grateful. I wanted to wake up early today—although maybe not this early—because I had a lot of things on my mind, and instead of curling up and moping about them, I wanted to do something about them.

First thing was first: Cheese's phone.

I was too tired and bummed out last night to spend much time on it, so I took advantage of the house still being asleep to study it and make a diagram of all its visible parts. There was the light-flower, which I knew from experience to be the power cell. Then there was the smooth part that sort of vibrated, which I thought must be kind of like the thing that houses the

RAM and stuff—or whatever Cheese's version of that would be. Beyond that, there wasn't much to sketch out. In the light of my desk lamp, the smooth part looked like a shell. But when I carried it over to the window, I could make out faint shapes etched in the surface. But as soon as my eye caught them, I lost them again, the light shifting or my hand changing the angle. I could never see them long enough to sketch out their shape. It was like trying to draw those floating things in your eyeballs that disappear as soon as you look at them.

I noticed another thing, though, in the light of the window. The slightest indentation at the very bottom of the smooth shell-shaped part. It was so subtle and shallow that I hadn't seen it before. It was like a baby's fingerprint in Play-Doh.

"Hmm," I said out loud. "What could that be?"

I drew it as a light gray oval on the diagram. It couldn't be a button because I pressed it every way I could think of. I even tried tapping on it like I was knocking on a tiny door. Nothing. I thought about how phones needed to charge, but with the light-flower growing, I figured it had plenty of power. I'd just started examining the phone again when I heard my dad calling up from downstairs that if I wanted to eat, I'd better hurry up. How was it time for breakfast already?! I had to hurry up for sure or the rest of my morning's plans would get derailed.

I threw on my clothes and then rushed down to the kitchen, ignoring Troy and his attempts to troll me, focusing instead on scarfing down the omelet that Dad had made. Mom was sipping her coffee silently. I kissed her cheek when I walked past because I knew she was still waking up and Mom didn't like anybody talking in too loud of a voice before she was all the way awake. And I almost always had too loud of a voice.

"Where you off to?" Dad asked when I was putting my dish in the sink.

"I was gonna stop by Mrs. McGee's house before school," I said, careful to not look up from where I was rinsing my plate. I was a terrible liar. I was positive he'd seen that I'd been eavesdropping right on my face. I felt more than a little guilty about it, but standing in the kitchen knowing they were thinking about selling the house . . . well, I felt a little mad, too.

"Oh?" Mom said. Her eyes looked more awake.

"Yeah," I said. "I want to make sure Handy-Bot 3.0 is still running smoothly."

"That's nice, son," Mom said. I went on avoiding their eyes as I gathered up my backpack and stuff and found my way to the door.

"Do you have your phone?"

"Yes, ma'am!" I called, and then I was out the door, glad that I managed to escape without giving anything away. I may not have been able to figure out everything about Cheese's device, but that was because I didn't have anyone to ask. For the question of my parents selling our house, I couldn't ask them, either. But maybe I could learn some things from Mrs. McGee.

Except when I started to climb the steps up to her yard from the sidewalk, it wasn't Mrs. McGee I saw. It was someone else. He was standing in the neighbor's yard next door to Mrs. McGee's and using a mallet to drive a sign into the ground.

FOR SALE, it read in big bright letters. JOIN THE NEW WAVE OF FERROUS CITY.

The new wave, I thought. *The new wave of what?*

I was going to ignore the man and go straight to Mrs. McGee's porch, but his voice caught at me before I even reached it.

"Are you looking for Mrs. McGee, young man?" he called. "She may not be home. I know she's been staying with a friend while the moving company packs everything up for her. Figured it would be a lot less stressful if someone else handled packing. She does stop by every now and then, though, so you're welcome to knock."

I paused, unsure of whether I should talk to him or not. He seemed to notice my hesitation because he laid the mallet down and reached in his pocket, pulling out a card.

"I'm Peter White," he said, passing it over the short fence between the yards. "I work in real estate. I helped Mrs. McGee sell her home and now I'm helping her neighbor sell his."

"*Everybody* is moving," I said, mostly to myself.

"Shifts in the market," he said. I groaned. Adults and their lingo, the kind that seemed like it didn't mean anything. A look must have crossed my face, because the man paused and cocked his head to the side. "Wait, a minute, are you Ethan?"

I didn't answer right away, knowing what my parents would say. But Mr. White seemed to be ready for that, too.

"I know, I know, stranger danger," he said. "But Mrs. McGee told me all about you and I just put two and two together. You're the famous inventor of Ferrous City!"

"I'm not famous," I said, blushing. "But I am an inventor."

"Famous, according to Mrs. McGee," he insisted. "She said you started up some kind of studio for inventors? At the old factory?"

"Yeah, that's right." I nodded. He knew a lot, so I believed that Mrs. McGee had told him stuff. But something about the way he asked questions made me feel uneasy. Like this wasn't a real conversation, but an experiment. It felt like he was gathering my answers with tweezers and putting them in jars.

"I'll bet you meet a lot of characters running a place like that," he said, leaning casually on the fence. "Especially with all these new folks moving into the city."

"There are a lot of new people," I said. "The same people buying these houses, I guess."

I didn't want to tell him my parents are considering selling our house. I didn't want him knowing any more about me than he already did. I held his real estate card in my hand. It seemed legit, but still, even realtors could be creeps.

"There's probably a lot of reasons a bunch of people decided to up and move to Ferrous City," he said, still leaning on the fence. "But I'm here to make sure everyone comfortably finds where they're supposed to be."

I frowned a little at that, confused.

"Realty is about more than finding a home for someone," he said, smiling. His smile seemed a little stiff. "It's also about knowing a neighborhood inside and out. If people are flocking to a certain area, then a realtor needs to know why. We need to know what makes an area tick. It helps when we can talk to people who live there. What would *you* say makes this area tick, Ethan?"

"Uh, um, I have no idea."

"Surely you know something," he pressed, still smiling. "New neighbors, new people at your school? Why do they say they've come to Ferrous City?"

"I don't know anybody new," I said.

"What about anyone who has left?" he said. "Any good friends who have moved away?"

"Um . . ."

"It's an interesting time to be in Ferrous City," he went on. "I'd love to know if you've noticed anything different."

"Ethan, is that you? What are you doing out in my yard at 7:30 in the morning?"

I whipped around and found Mrs. McGee standing out on her front porch in her robe, peering across the yard at me and Mr. White.

"Oh, she *is* home!" Mr. White grinned, and turned to leave. "Lucky."

He was gone before I even got to Mrs. McGee's porch.

A WHOLE COLLECTION OF THINGS TO WORRY ABOUT

"Who was that?" Mrs. McGee said to me, welcoming me with a half hug.

"Your realtor," I said.

"Was it?" she said. "He looks different every time I see him. Sometimes a hat, sometimes a coat. You know, to these old eyes everyone starts to look the same after a while."

"I heard that you're moving, Mrs. McGee."

"Oh, did you now? Well, I'm sorry you had to hear it through the grapevine. I was going to drop off a caramel cake before I went, though, I promise you that. I wasn't just going to up and disappear."

"Looks like your neighbors are moving, too."

She leaned over the porch to read the sign Mr. White had hammered into the yard.

"Appears to be so. They're getting old like me. Sick of the upkeep maybe."

"Is that really why you're leaving?" I asked. "I kind of hoped Handy-Bot would help you take care of things."

"Oh, sure," she said, smiling fondly. "That robot of yours is a great help. But there's only so much it can do when it comes to cutting grass and trimming hedges. Plus, this neighborhood is changing. It doesn't feel like home anymore, Ethan. So busy and I hear they'll be raising property taxes, what with that fancy new company opening and home prices going up. That doesn't mean anything to you, of course. But I know when it's time to fold. At least I got a good price."

I nodded, even though I didn't fully understand. Sure, the neighborhood felt different. But it was almost like Mrs. McGee could see into the future, like she knew the ways that it was changing weren't the only ways it would change. Mr. White seemed to know something about that, too, but he was interested in a different way than Mrs. McGee.

"Shouldn't you be getting to school, Ethan?" she said, nudging me. "I came out to get my paper and I saw you! I'm glad you stopped by to see me. I'll bring that cake by in a few days."

"Yes ma'am, I'm going. I just wanted to check in on Handy-Bot. Maybe I'll give it an upgrade before you leave so it can do more around the yard."

"Thank you, Ethan," Mrs. McGee said in a warm voice. "That'd be lovely."

I waved goodbye and walked the rest of the way to school, but it was hard to be lost in thought when I was noticing so many things that were new about the neighborhood. COMING SOON signs in store windows for things like specialty coffee and a restaurant called Kung Fu Tofu. Mrs. McGee was right. It didn't feel like home. I wasn't sure *what* it felt like. And it felt like it was happening so fast.

I was so distracted that I walked more slowly than usual. It wasn't until I saw how few people were walking into school that I realized I was late! I dashed the rest of the way, slowing down only slightly on my way down the hall.

Mr. Hardin gave me a stern look as I reached for the door. I had never been late in my life! Whatever was clouding up my head needed to clear out, and fast.

"You're quiet, dude," Kareem said after school, when he, Juan Carlos, and I were making our way to the Create Space. "Are you still bummed out you got a tardy slip?"

I hadn't been thinking about it, but the reminder made me mad all over again.

"I'd forgotten all about it until now. Thanks a lot," I said. I tried to make it a joke, but Kareem could tell otherwise.

"Then what's the problem?" he said.

"Why are you asking me?" I said. "I'm not the only one who's quiet. Ask Juan Carlos. Juan Carlos, why are *you* so quiet?"

"I'm worried about my parents passing their citizenship test," he said. I stopped walking right in the middle of the sidewalk.

"I remember you talking about that," I said. "They're taking it now?"

"No, not yet," he said. "They've been studying for months. Studying like all the time. At breakfast, at dinner. I've been helping them and doing all the things I can think of to make sure they pass. And they know everything. But it doesn't mean they'll pass. My tía got every question right except one and they decided to tell her no. So she has to try again. I don't want that to happen to my parents. I'm so proud of them and I think it would make them feel ashamed if they didn't pass. And they shouldn't be."

"What about your abuela?" Kareem said. "Did she already take it?"

"Yeah, and she passed. She's helping them study, too. Everyone says they're going to do fine and it's going to be a breeze but I'm nervous, you know? We all live together now and I want it to stay that way."

Juan Carlos didn't say a whole lot most of the time, and definitely never this much all at once. And definitely never anything this serious. I could tell he'd had something on his mind lately—he was usually so goofy and he'd been so serious lately. But I hadn't known how to ask, so I'd just left it alone. I thought about how Fatima nominated him to be our group leader. I wondered if she could tell that he had things to say, and if that was why she said he should be the leader.

"That's a lot," Kareem said. "I'm sorry you and your family are stressing."

"Me, too," I added. "Is there anything we can do to help?"

"Nah," Juan Carlos said. "I'm just gonna keep helping them study and pray a lot."

He'd never talked about praying before, either. I guess he'd mentioned church, but I didn't even know where he went to church. I reminded myself to say a little prayer for his family, too.

"Wow, it's busy," Juan Carlos said, pointing ahead at the Create Space. He was right. There was a crowd of people heading inside. But I could also tell he was trying to change the subject. I wanted to say something, but my mom says that sometimes being quiet and listening is the best help you can be.

"Are we going to work on the project?" Kareem said.

"Yes," I answered. "But we need to figure out a way to involve Fatima while still keeping Cheese and the device a secret. Ms. Erivo said that Fatima told her I wasn't involving her and the last thing I need is Ms. Erivo getting too close."

"She looks pretty involved," Kareem said, pointing. "Look."

We had just stepped inside the Create Space and the first thing I saw was Fatima leaning against a table where some people from school were working on their science project. She was laughing and smiling and gesturing with her hands like she'd been part of this school since kindergarten.

"What is *she* doing here?" I growled under my breath. "How does she even know about this place?"

"Everybody knows about this place," Kareem laughed, shoving me lightly. "What do you mean? She probably walked over with Attica and them."

Attica seemed to be who she was talking to the most, so Kareem was probably right. But still, something in my stomach sizzled. Maybe we could get to an empty table without her seeing us. The last thing I needed was to be slowed down explaining the last summer to Fatima because she caught us whispering.

Not a chance.

"Hey, I didn't know y'all were coming up here today," Fatima said, appearing at our table. We'd only sat down five minutes before. Her face looked concerned. "Are you working on our project without me?"

"Uh, no," I said. I was glad I hadn't yet pulled out my science stuff. "We're, um, working on something else. Something we started over the summer."

"Oh," she said, brightening. "What is it?"

"Nothing," I said quickly. She looked a little hurt and I felt bad about it. But keeping Cheese a secret was important—way more important than the new kid who bragged a lot on the first day of school.

"How do you like school?" Kareem asked her. I kicked him under the table. We needed her to leave, not stay and chat!

"It's nice," she said. "I'm not used to such a small town, but it's cool. Pretty much everyone is friendly."

I knew right away that I was not included in her "pretty much everyone" but I didn't care. And she didn't even look at me. She asked Kareem about what he said for his fun fact—that he'd switched schools and then switched back—and they started having their own conversation, making me madder and madder. We came to brainstorm ways to unlock Cheese's phone! Not waste time talking to the most annoying girl in class!

"Well," she said, finally wrapping up after what felt like half an hour. "Let me know when you guys are ready to start working on our project. We shouldn't wait too long."

"It's only like the second day of school," Kareem said, laughing.

"Time flies!" she shrugged.

"Let me guess," I said, my frustration spilling through my voice. "You have a patent on a flying machine."

Any chance someone wouldn't catch my anger ends about a second after I spoke. No one laughed. Not Kareem, not Juan Carlos. As for Fatima, well . . .

Some people would shoot me a look and ignore me, but Fatima didn't do that. She stared at me for a long time, like she was waiting for me to explain why I'd said it. A whole different silence than my friends were giving me. My stomach sank.

"Good luck on your project, guys," she said eventually and then left.

Once she was gone, I was left with the real silence, the real looks from my friends. And they weren't happy with me.

"What the heck, Ethan?" Kareem muttered.

"What?" I demanded. "We have work to do!"

"Yeah, but did you have to be like that to her?"

I looked pleadingly to Juan Carlos to back me up, but even he was too busy staring at his own hands to offer a third opinion. And, okay, maybe I was a little harsh. But I'll bet if Fatima knew the weight of what she had interrupted just to talk to Kareem about everyday stuff, she would've done what I did. The road to helping Cheese wasn't an easy one.

"Can we talk about it later?" I pleaded. "Cheese might be in trouble and I can be nicer to Fatima whenever."

Kareem exhaled. "Okay."

With the buzz of the Create Space in the background, we finally got down to it. All the problems in my life outside this table seemed to melt away. Things would be so much better if this was the only thing I had to worry about.

MAKE AMENDS?

After the first day of school, I'd learned to be as quick as possible at my locker. Fatima's locker was two down from mine, and I didn't want to risk being around her. But since two days ago at the Create Space, it was like a mosquito had bitten me inside my brain and it kept itching whenever I thought about Fatima. The feeling reminded me of the time when I was like five and I had found a toy soldier on the playground and I took it home, even though I'd seen the kid who was playing with it earlier. I felt sick until I went back to the playground and put the toy where I found it. And the next time I saw the kid, he had it again. And then I felt better.

When I got to school, I didn't rush at my locker. I opened it slowly, giving it two sharp tugs, which was the trick. I even took my time getting my stuff out. But Fatima didn't show. I wondered if she was home sick. I felt disappointed and I didn't even know why: It wasn't like I knew what I was going to say to her. *Sorry you're my least favorite person. I just find you very annoying?*

While I waited, I thought and thought about ways to make Cheese's phone work. Kareem and Juan Carlos and I had stayed at the Create Space for hours and we made a list of all the things a phone might need to turn on. But when I got home and checked out the device, none of our ideas worked. I was getting so frustrated I started to regret suggesting this science project. Even if we got a great grade on our research of deep-space communication, it would still feel like a failure if we never got to talk to Cheese.

Things got worse in Ms. Erivo's class when we were given time to work on our group project.

"I found a couple studies last night when I was researching," Fatima said, leaning in. "About the Deep Space Stations and what they're finding. They have all this data we can cite . . ."

I had been racking my brains all morning and this wasn't going to help me unlock Cheese's phone.

I turned to Juan Carlos and Kareem. "Do you have to go straight home after school? I want to talk to you about something."

"Shouldn't we be talking now?" Fatima said, raising her eyebrow.

75

I hadn't realized that I had interrupted her. Everything from the Create Space flooded back. Now's as good a time as any to try being a little nicer.

"Sorry, Fatima," I said impatiently. "I just need to talk to Kareem and Juan Carlos for a minute."

Fatima sighed loudly, giving us permission, and Kareem and Juan Carlos leaned in.

"What's the deal? Is something wrong?" Kareem asked.

I whispered as low as I could so Fatima wouldn't overhear. "I still haven't managed to get Cheese's phone unlocked, and I don't know . . . I'm getting a weird feeling. Like all these new people in Ferrous City. There was this guy outside Mrs. McGee's and he says he was a realtor but he was asking questions about newcomers and people who left. It just felt . . . off. I'd really like to make sure Cheese is okay, you know?"

They both looked concerned and not dismissive, so that was a relief. I had felt kind of silly, being so suspicious. But it just felt too familiar. Strangers walking around Ferrous City and pretending to be normal people.

"Uh-hem," Fatima chimed in. She was right, we had to get back to class.

"I'll tell you guys the rest after school," I whispered to Juan Carlos and Kareem. Of course, after science, the rest of the day crawled along like a slug.

Just one more class. I closed my locker and headed toward math. I had only gotten a few feet when I heard a familiar voice coming from around the corner. When I reached it, I found Fatima having a heated debate with Jodie, the sole member of the AHA society. Wow, it was like every second of this day got more annoying!

"It sounds like confirmation bias to me," Fatima was saying with her arms crossed. "All the examples you're giving could be interpreted any way, but you're looking at them from an angle that confirms what you want to believe."

"Not believing there is life outside Earth is stupidity," Jodie said. He sounded peeved. "This is why we haven't invited any girls to AHA."

"Excuse me?" Fatima said.

"Excuse me?!" I said. They turned to look at me, surprised.

"What?" Jodie said, confused.

"Did you just call Fatima *stupid*?" I snapped. "Don't you know she has two patents? Just because someone doesn't believe aliens exist—"

"And I didn't even *say* that," Fatima interrupted, glaring at Jodie. "I said there was no convincing proof. He was talking about beliefs and I was just arguing that belief is different than fact."

"Basic science," I said to Jodie, giving him a dirty look. He squinted back at me like he was changing his mind about trying to get me to join AHA, which made me make my look even dirtier. Defending Fatima wasn't high on my list of things to do, but joining AHA was even lower. And besides, calling someone stupid who obviously isn't stupid is ridiculous. Name calling in general just isn't cool.

"Everyone needs to be getting to class now," Mr. Hardin called down the hall, clapping his hands.

Jodie spun around and disappeared down the hall.

"That was annoying," Fatima said. She tucked her hair behind her ear and shook her head. We set off down the hallway, too.

"I'm sorry he was a jerk," I said.

"Funny to hear you call someone a jerk," she said, laughing. "Of all people."

I almost tripped when she said that, but I kept walking.

"I'm not a jerk!" I cried.

"Yes, you are," she said.

"Ugh, maybe you're right," I said as we arrived at the classroom door.

"Why *have* you been so mean?" she said in a demanding voice. It made me want to be mean again, but then I'd just be proving her point.

I shrugged. "I don't know! I'm just—"

"Jealous," she said. She stared me straight in my eyes like my mom did sometimes. I squirmed.

"I'm not jealous."

"Yes, you are. You're an inventor, too, and you wanted to be the only inventor. But it doesn't have to be a competition. Why do boys always make everything a competition?"

"It's not just boys!" I protested.

"True," she said. "But it feels like it sometimes. Especially when it comes to being smart."

"Okay, well, I'm sorry," I said again. "I wasn't trying to be mean. And I wasn't trying to be jealous. I was just . . . I don't know. I have a lot on my mind, okay! There's a lot going on!"

"Like our science project," she said. "If you'd let me help, then maybe I could *help!*"

I bit my lip. We were getting too close to the truth, and if I admitted that I was having trouble with the project, then she'd demand to help. But if I didn't admit it, she'd probably still demand to help. Why did she have to be in our group to begin with?!

I sighed and threw my head back.

"What is the *problem*, Ethan?" she cried. "You act like the group project is a secret between you and the boys! Like you're worried I'm going to steal it—"

"I'm not worried about that," I huffed.

"But you are worried about *something*," she said quickly.

"Yes, but—"

"But what?"

"This is about a lot more than a project for school, okay!" I whispered furiously. "You think it's just about Ms. Erivo's class, but it's so much more than that."

She crossed her arms in the same cocky way she did with Jodie.

"Why are you making this so difficult?" I cried.

"I'm not doing anything!" she said.

Teachers began calling for everyone to clear the halls, but Fatima must have seen something on my face because she took a step closer and put a reassuring hand on my shoulder.

"What is it, Ethan? We're in this together."

And that was when I decided to trust her. Because it's not every day that you meet a sixth grader with two patents, and we needed all the help we could get with figuring out the best way to use Cheese's communication device—especially in a way that kept him safe. But bringing Fatima in on the secret of the device meant bringing her in on the secret of everything. It meant walking her through the whole summer and the whole story, and it wasn't just my story to tell.

I was nervous, the same type of nervous as when I saw the Others walking down my neighborhood's streets in their suits. The scary feeling of not knowing who you could trust. I definitely couldn't make this decision on my own.

"Okay, fine," I said. "There is something happening with the science project. I can't say what, at least not here. If you think I can trust you with absolute secrecy—and I mean *absolute*—then meet me and Juan Carlos and Kareem by the stream down the hill from the Create Space today after school. Don't bring anyone with you, and don't tell anyone you're meeting us."

"This doesn't sound safe," she said doubtfully.

I rolled my eyes.

"Oh, please. If I really wanted to hurt you, I'd wait until our first big test and tell Ms. Erivo you plagiarized something."

Her eyes widened.

"How dare you," she said.

"I wouldn't do that!" I snapped. "Never to a fellow scientist!"

Something shifted between us, something very tiny, but it was there. I didn't want to read too much into it. After all, she might still be just as annoying at the end of the day. But four heads were better than three, and when it came to reaching out across the stars to Cheese, we needed all the help we could get.

12

NO MORE SECRETS

"So, wait, let me get this straight," Kareem said as we paced beside the creek while waiting for Fatima. "You bent over backwards trying to keep Fatima from finding out about Cheese and the communication device. You didn't even want to work with her on the science project. And now you're bringing her in on everything? You're just going to tell her?"

"Well, that's why I had you guys meet me here first," I said. "Because I wanted to ask if you think we should."

"Why now?" Juan Carlos said, considering.

"Because we're kind of hitting a dead end," I sighed. "It seems to have power but I can't get it to turn on. Like it's in sleep mode or something. We've tried everything! And I just . . . need to know that Cheese is okay."

I kicked a branch and it went spinning off into the creek. I thought back to the day we were down here gathering junk, trying to figure out a way to make Cheese's ship work. We thought we had tried everything then, too. I knew we could figure this out.

"Fatima is smart," Kareem said. "Probably even smarter than you, Ethan, but—"

"Hey!" I cried.

"Oh, relax," Kareem said. "You don't always have to be the smartest. But her being really smart isn't the issue, is it? It's whether we can trust her."

I nodded. That was exactly the issue. I trusted my brothers and they didn't even know about Cheese. I trusted my parents, and they didn't know, either. I had been thinking about it ever since my conversation with Fatima. It was like there were different kinds of trust. Even though Jodie believed in aliens, I didn't trust him with information about Cheese. And even though I barely knew Fatima at all, the fact that she was skeptical about aliens somehow made me trust her more. I just hoped I wasn't wrong.

"She doesn't seem like she'd go running around telling everyone," Kareem said. "But you can never tell about a person. She's new here. What if she told a bunch of people, hoping to make friends?"

"She wouldn't," Juan Carlos said confidently. "She's not the type to want people to like her for silly reasons."

Kareem and I both nodded. None of us knew Fatima well, but we knew Juan Carlos was right about her. She just wasn't that type of kid.

"I think it will be okay," I said, not very convincingly.

We stood silently for a minute, looking at the sky, our heads tilted back. Like even when we weren't purposefully thinking about Cheese, we were still looking for him.

"What are you looking at?" Fatima called.

We all jerked our heads down from space and found her inching her way down the steep path that led to the creek's edge. She had changed into rain boots, which was impressive. She plans ahead.

"Nothing," Juan Carlos said. "We were all just thinking."

"About what lies you're going to tell me next?" she said. We were all kind of shocked, but she didn't say it accusingly. Just matter-of-factly. "Or have you brought me here to tell me what it is you three have been working on without me?"

Even though her attitude still made me kind of mad, I also kind of appreciated it. You didn't have to guess with Fatima. She told it to you straight.

"We've been discussing it," I said as she finished climbing down the slope. "And yes, I think we're ready to tell you the truth. But like I said at school, only if you are committed to the utmost secrecy."

"Well, it depends," she said.

"What do you mean it *depends*?" I cried.

"There are factors that affect whether secrecy is okay," she shrugged. "Like, is it the kind of secret that someone would be hurt by? Ethics are important in science."

I stared at her, stunned. "No one is going to get hurt," I cried. "I wouldn't keep that kind of secret."

She smiled. "That's good to know. So why does it have to be a secret? What are the stakes?"

"Someone could get hurt if people *knew* about the secret," Juan Carlos said, and I nodded. "The secret protects them."

"Protects who?"

"That's part of the secret," I snapped.

"You always get mad when people ask you things," she said, sighing. "It's annoying."

Kareem snickered and I whipped my head around to glare at him. Annoying? Me? She was the annoying one! I was starting to regret inviting her here to begin with.

"Look," she said. "If you say keeping the secret keeps the person from getting hurt, then I think I'm okay keeping it."

"Okay," Kareem said slowly. "The only thing is, it's not exactly a person."

"What isn't?" she said with a confused face.

"Um, the person we're protecting isn't exactly a person."

"Oh," she said. "So, is this about animal rights? I know some fields of science still really struggle . . ."

But she trailed off. Our faces told her that she was on the wrong track.

"What?" she said.

I took a deep breath. Fatima always gave it to you straight, so I figured I would try and do that, too.

"Okay, so here's the thing," I said. "Over the summer, an alien landed here in Ferrous City. Its name was Cheese. Kareem and Juan Carlos and I helped fix its ship and get it back out into space before the creatures hunting Cheese tracked the alien down. We kind of all became friends. And we miss Cheese.

"It turns out, Cheese left a communication device under my bed powered by light-flowers, and we're trying to study the device and figure out how to turn it on so we can call outer space. But we've been hitting dead end after dead end. And . . . well, you're smart. And we think we can trust you to not tell anyone so no one can track Cheese down. So . . . yeah. That's it."

The woods down by the creek were quiet. All I heard was the gentle trickling sound of the water over a tiny water-fall. And then the sound of Fatima laughing.

"Wow, you brought me all the way down here for this?" she said, shaking her head. "If you wanted to try to prank me, you could've just done it in the hall with Jodie. Is this like a tradition of yours or something? What a joke."

She turned away, ready to climb the bank back up to the hiking path. Kareem and Juan Carlos and I looked at each other. I knew that her not believing us would be a possibility.

If I hadn't met Cheese, I probably wouldn't have believed me, either.

"What if I can show you proof?" I called to her. "That's what you said in the hallway, right? That you would believe something if there were proof? Scientific evidence?"

She stopped in her tracks, then slowly turned back to face us.

"What kind of evidence?"

"I brought the communication device," I said. Kareem and Juan Carlos looked at me in surprise. I hadn't told them that I was bringing it, but I wanted to have it with me just in case. I didn't like having it outside the safety of my room, but I was going straight home after this.

"You brought the supposed alien communication device, and you have it with you right now?" she said. She sounded sarcastic but I could also sense the curiosity in her voice. I recognized the fellow scientist in her. I smiled a little.

"Yes," I said. "I have it right here in my bag. Do you want to see it?"

She didn't respond, but she did start walking back toward us. I figured that was an answer. I reached into my bag and gently pulled Cheese's device into the light.

I tried to remember how I felt the first time I saw the light-flowers, the way they moved and dazzled like nothing I had ever seen. I think my face probably looked a lot like Fatima's looked right now.

"What in the . . . ?" she breathed, then reached out a hand. "Can I touch it?"

"Sure," I said. I didn't have to tell her to be careful. She was a scientist, and her touch was light and delicate.

"Wow," she said. "I was wondering if this would be real or . . ."

"Or what?" Kareem said. "You really thought we'd go this far to try to play a prank on you?"

Fatima barely glanced up at us as she examined the light-flower. Which, of course, was better than her getting upset at us like before, but I wished we could get a bit more of her attention. Make sure we were all together on this.

"I was wondering if it would be real or if you three had lost your marbles," she said, still staring at the light-flower. "If you three were part of a mass delusion event or something. You've heard about those, right?"

She trailed off, engrossed in Cheese's phone. If Kareem and Juan Carlos and I had lost our marbles, it was clear that Fatima was now losing hers, too. And that meant we were on the same team.

13

INTRUDER!!!

I took the long way on the walk home to clear my mind. Between trying to figure out how to talk to Cheese, managing the Create Space, and adjusting to a new grade, my head was spinning. But there was one bright spot: Fatima.

I felt so much better after showing her the light-flower phone. Maybe it was silly not to trust her initially. I remember not trusting Juan Carlos at first and he turned out to be one of the best friends I've ever had. Besides, having the extra brainpower may be just the thing I need to solve my Cheese problem.

When I got home, I headed to the kitchen to make a peanut-butter and marshmallow sandwich. My FAVOR-ITE! There's nothing like a freshly toasted PB&M after a long day, and a cold glass of milk to wash it down. I put my bread in the toaster and began gathering my ingredients.

BADOOMP!

A thud coming from upstairs stopped me in my tracks.

"Hello!?" I called out. Nobody replied.

I knew my family was out because everyone's car was gone and all the lights were out, except for the stove light I'd just turned on.

"Hellooo!?" I yelled again. Still no reply.

SHMWOP!

My bread popped out of the toaster, and I nearly popped out of my socks. I stayed still, barely breathing, listening. After a long silent wait, I figured the wind must've knocked something over.

Climp-clomp, climp-clomp, climp-clomp.

My heart almost jumped out of my chest. That wasn't something falling. That was someone walking. And it sounded like they were headed downstairs and straight for me!

Who could be in my house?! A cop? A stranger? An intruder? I didn't want to stick around and find out.

My first thought was to dash out the front door, but I'd have to pass the staircase and risk running right into the intruder. I thought about going out the back, but I'd be stuck in the backyard with nowhere to hide. That didn't seem like the safest option.

The footsteps grew closer.

I panicked and dove into the pantry closet. Instantly I regretted not making my move out the back door.

Climp-clomp, climp-clomp, climp-clomp.

The footsteps came closer. With every footfall, I clenched my fist tighter by my side. Suddenly I felt something in my pocket. My phone!

I took out my phone, but the screen didn't light up. I pressed around, but nothing happened.

"Jeez Louise," I whispered to myself. My phone was dead.

I peeked through the shutter doors of the pantry. A dark figure scurried into the kitchen. Whoever it was wasn't that tall. They may have even been shorter than me, but wider for sure.

I leaned to the side, trying to get a glimpse of them, but they weren't in my line of sight. I could hear the intruder sniffing around my peanut butter and marshmallows, though. I clinched my fists even tighter. Nobody messes with my PB&M.

I looked around to see what I could use to protect myself. In the corner, I noticed a wooden push broom. Slowly, and being careful not to make a sound, I put my foot on the base of the broom and unscrewed the long handle, clutching it as best as I could. If I was going down, I wasn't going down without a fight.

While the intruder was distracted, I nudged open the pantry doors and slipped out. Sometimes being slim comes in handy.

I couldn't make out the intruder in the darkness of the house, but I didn't want to spend too much time staring, either. I had a plan to execute. Phase one: Get out of this kitchen!

I dipped down, close to the floor so I couldn't be seen behind the kitchen island, then I duck-walked toward the back door. My heart was pounding so loudly I thought the stranger would hear it. I closed my eyes tightly with every step, hoping not to hit the wrong part of the floor and make a creak or a crack or a crunch. When I turned the corner, I was out of sight, and could breathe again. I stood up and hurried to execute phase two of my plan: Set a decoy.

When I reached the back door, I fumbled with the locks, trying to get the door open. Why did it have so many locks!?

Creeakkk.

As the back door opened, a loud squeak echoed through the house, followed by a rustling in the kitchen. The intruder had heard me!

I threw the wooden broom handle as far as I could and before it even hit the ground, I dove behind a window curtain and put my hands over my mouth to keep from exhaling.

Climp-clomp, climp-clomp.

The intruder came racing around the corner just as the flying broom handle crashed into the garbage cans. Then, suddenly, they took off out the back door.

I sprang out from behind the curtain and raced to shut the door.

I locked all the locks and flipped the switch for the back porch light. I ran through the house, grabbing my phone charger on the way, and reached for the front door. But right as my hand grabbed it, the knob started to turn from the other side. All I could do was back up and yell as the door flung open.

"AGGGHHHHHHHH—"

"What in the world is the matter?" my dad said as he walked in the house.

I don't think I've ever been happier to see my dad.

"Dad! Quick in the back, someone's there."

My dad dropped his bags and rushed to the coat closet to grab a wooden bat.

"Stay here," he said sternly.

And I did. My dad was a big guy. I figured he could handle the intruder all on his own. If he needed backup, I'm sure he'd call, but I really hoped he didn't.

Never in a million years would I think we'd have a home invader. But ever since Cheese landed here, things have been getting weirder and weirder.

"Ethan!" Dad called out. Without thinking, I hurried to the back of the house to be at my dad's side.

When I got there, he was standing in the doorway with the broom handle I'd thrown.

"I'm not sure what you saw but I didn't see anyone back here. Mind explaining this, though?" he asked, handing me the stick. Only it was broken in half and one of the tips was covered in goo. I held the handle closer to get a better look. I instantly recognized the slimy substance. It looked just like the goo we saw coming from the squished light-thieves.

"Another one of your experiments, I presume?" my dad said, breaking my concentration.

I was so caught off guard, I didn't know what to say.

"Uhhh, yes, sorry. I'll get this cleaned up, Dad."

"And the marshmallows you spilled all over the counter?"

I craned my neck around the corner and saw marshmallows everywhere. More havoc caused by the alien intruder.

"Yep, I'm on it," I said politely. "But you didn't see anything else?" I asked, peering out the back door.

"Nope, I checked everywhere. Maybe you heard a stray cat or something."

"Yeah, maybe so," I said, sounding unsure, but not meaning to.

"It's okay, son," my dad said, giving me a reassuring pat on the head as he headed back toward the kitchen. "Go ahead and get cleaned up, I'm gonna need some help prepping for the block party tomorrow."

But I couldn't move. I was stuck in my tracks, staring at the goo on the broomstick. I'd have to run some tests, but if my hypothesis was correct, a light-thief had just broken into my house. But why? How? As much as I wanted to tell my dad, I couldn't. I wasn't even sure I could tell my friends, I didn't want to put them in danger. This was something I needed to face alone.

BLOCK PARTY TIME

The next morning, I woke to the sound of my brother cheering. It was early and I heard my dad shout at him from his room.

"Troy! What are you carrying on about?"

"Mr. Elder just called and said he's closing the store for the block party! I can go!"

He cheered again. My mom yelled at him through the wall, too, but I knew she was happy. We went to the block party as a family every year and she was sad that Troy wasn't going to be able to join us. I found myself smiling. It wouldn't have been the same without all of us together. That said, this year I planned to break off from them to check out the party on my own. Juan Carlos, Kareem, and I had plans. I wondered if they were awake. I grabbed my phone, used my face ID to unlock it, and then I sent them a group text.

Are you guys ready for today?

Surprisingly enough, Juan Carlos answered right away: *Of course. I have something I want you guys to try.*

Then Kareem a little later: *I'm definitely ready! Leave the you-know-what at home, though, Ethan.*

I rolled my eyes. *Obviously.*

There was no reason to bring Cheese's communication device. Fatima had already inspected it and said she would do some thinking about how she could possibly get it to work. She had made sketches in a tiny notebook, which I thought was cool because that's what I do, too, when I'm trying to solve a problem. We told her about the block party, but she already had plans, which was kind of disappointing. I was hoping she might have some stuff to tell us. But I needed a rest from thinking about the device anyway. Sometimes you can only make a breakthrough if you let your mind focus on something else. And the block party was the perfect thing to focus on.

By the time we got to the block party, it was already in full swing. My parents went straight to the shopping section. Tons of sellers from all over Ferrous City set up booths along the street. When I was little, I would have to trail my parents from booth to booth while they looked at art and stuff, but now that I was a little older, they told us where to meet them and at what time.

"You have a phone now," my mom said, pointing at me. "Keep track of the time and call if you need us."

"Yes, ma'am," I said, and then I ran off toward the food carts to meet Juan Carlos and Kareem.

Juan Carlos had something in each hand and Kareem had one, too. It was corn on the cob in a little paper cradle. But it had stuff on it—sauce and seasonings.

"Elotes," Juan Carlos said happily, handing one to me. "They're one of my favorite things. A block party isn't complete without elotes."

I held the stick and took a bite. It was delicious—salty cheese, tangy mayo, and the perfect hit of spice.

The three of us walked around, eating elotes and checking out food carts. Kareem bought churros, which we ate while watching the carnival game booths. There were more people this year than I remembered from past block parties. And more police. Usually, it's pretty laid-back and there are spontaneous dance parties and stuff, but it felt stiffer this year; like an event instead of a party.

"I cannot leave this table until I knock them all down in one turn," Kareem announced. I knew that tone. His competitive voice. When it came to things like cards or arcade stuff, Kareem and Juan Carlos couldn't stop until they'd won.

"In the meantime," I said, "I'm gonna go throw away our trash."

"Thanks, Ethan," they said in unison. They each gave the lady running the Balloon-a-Pult another dollar.

I shook my head and turned away, walking toward a recycling bin to dump our cardboard and sticks from the elotes. I was just tossing them inside when I heard someone saying my name.

"Ethan, is that you? So good to see you again so soon."

I turned to see Peter White, the realtor I'd met at Mrs. McGee's house. He was wearing the same outfit as before, smiling at me in that fake way.

"Hey, Mr. White," I said.

"Please, Peter is fine. Isn't this a wonderful day for a party?"

"Yeah, it definitely is," I said. I moved to go back toward where Kareem and Juan Carlos were still frantically lobbing water balloons with the help of an elastic belt. But Peter stretched his hand out to get my attention.

"I wondered if you had thought any more about Ferrous City," he said. "About what makes it tick."

"Um, no, I hadn't really had a chance to think about it, sorry," I said. "I've been busy with school and stuff."

That weird feeling was back. Something wasn't right about this guy.

"Of course, of course," he said. "Silly me. Do your teachers ever talk about this sort of thing? Learning more about your city? What draws people to it? There seems to be something special about Ferrous City, and I'm curious about what it might be."

"You mean so you can sell people houses here?" I asked.

He paused, studying me. "Yes," he said. "Precisely."

"Have my parents talked to you about selling our house?" I asked him suddenly. I realized I couldn't ask my parents, but what if they had already started the process? I wanted to know. I also wanted to see if he would even answer.

Peter's eyes fixed on me with interest.

"Are your parents looking to move?" he asked. "No, they haven't spoken to me, but I'd be more than happy to talk to them."

"No, no, it's okay," I said quickly. "I was just wondering."

"Curiosity is a good thing," he answered. "I'm curious, too."

"Uhh, I'm curious about what that guy is doing over there," I said, pointing over his shoulder. Peter White turned to look, and I quickly walked in the opposite direction. I felt bad about it, and super awkward, but I didn't know how else to get out of the conversation. When I looked back over my shoulder, Peter was gone.

"Watch out, Ethan!" someone said, right as I walked into them.

I stumbled back and realized it was Jodie. *Great.*

"Have you heard?" Jodie said in an excited voice. He didn't seem mad about our recent run-in with Fatima.

"About what?" I asked.

"That there's intel about aliens having been present in Ferrous City as recently as two days ago," he said.

It felt like a stone dropped in my stomach.

"Huh?"

"Yes," Jodie said, nodding fast. "Someone on the chat boards said that their alien material scanner pinged on Thursday."

My mind raced, wondering if any of it was true. *Alien material scanner?* I'd never heard of such a thing, but I imagined it could detect an extraterrestrial presence, like a PB&M sandwich destroying light-thief.

"Weird," I said, thinking fast. "I was just looking for you. I overheard a very interesting conversation that I thought you should know about."

I leaned in, trying to look secretive. Jodie leaned in, too; I had clearly piqued his curiosity.

"I was in the bathroom at City Hall yesterday," I said. I picked City Hall because it sounded official. I didn't even know where City Hall *was.* "And I heard two people saying that they had received intel that there was a sighting of alien activity in Aiken, the next town over. Apparently, it happens every night at 10:22 p.m. and they're tracking it secretly. They said they've transferred all their units to Aiken because

Ferrous City had gone quiet. Most of the high activity is in Aiken now. But you didn't hear it from me, okay? I don't want to get in trouble."

I doubted he'd believe me, but Jodie's eyes lit up with excitement and determination.

"I could be there before ten," Jodie said to himself, forgetting that I was there. *Excuse me*, I wanted to say, *You're welcome!* But I bit my tongue as Jodie hustled out of the block party. I wondered if his parents were into aliens, too. They must have been. A family hobby. Where were his parents?

I made my way back to Kareem and Juan Carlos. With Peter and AHA both evaded, maybe I could go back to enjoying the block party.

"There is no way I'm going to let you win again," Kareem crowed, loading another balloon.

"You don't have a choice!" Juan Carlos yelled.

I watched them, smiling, as they launched water balloon after water balloon. They didn't care if it hit the target in the booth—each one was just trying to empty out his basket faster than the other.

"How many does he have left, Ethan?" Kareem said. "I can't take my eyes off to look!"

"Uh—"

"Don't tell him, Ethan!" Juan Carlos shouted.

"Let me just . . ." I moved forward to peek at both of their baskets. They both blocked me at the same time. Each of their balloons slipped from the catapults and burst on the ground.

We all got drenched.

"It's in my shoes!" Kareem wailed.

"My socks feel like sponges!" I cried.

"Oh, lugnuts," Juan Carlos said.

Kareem and I both stopped, turning to look at him.

"Lugnuts?" Kareem said.

"Lugnuts?" the woman running the booth said.

"Lugnuts?" I repeated.

Juan Carlos stared back and forth between us.

"It's time for another elote," he said.

A SPECIFIC KIND OF CRYING

The block party had an endless supply of elotes, which was both good and bad. Good, because now that Juan Carlos had introduced me to them, I was never going to stop eating them. Bad, because I was never going to stop eating them. Kareem was on the same page, and after we had played every game the block party had to offer, we decided to find a shady place to sit and hang out. I texted my mom and told her the plan. She gave a thumbs-up reply. I felt older, and as we settled onto a bench at the edge of the event, I decided I liked that feeling.

"How's it going with your parents?" I asked Juan Carlos. "Studying for their test?"

"I think they know everything they're supposed to know," he said. "But you know how it is when you take a test . . . sometimes everything you think you know flies out of your head."

That didn't happen to me often, but it definitely had happened. I bet it was even worse as an adult. And what about who was giving the test? Some teachers graded fair and let little mistakes slide if they could tell you did your best and had a brain fart. But some teachers seemed to enjoy being unfair and mark you off for every little thing. What if Juan Carlos's parents had someone like that marking the test?

"They're probably stressed out," I said. I thought about my parents, too. "Like, my parents are already thinking about how they're going to pay for college and stuff for me. Your parents are probably thinking about that, too, *plus* passing this test."

Juan Carlos nodded, looking worried.

"They've had temporary visas for years," he said. "I forgot they didn't have citizenship. But I know they never forgot. I just want everything to be okay. All of us here together."

"What happens if they don't pass?" Kareem asked quietly.

"I'm not exactly sure," Juan Carlos said. "I just know that we moved to Ferrous City so they could work and we could afford to live together. I don't know what it will be like if that changes."

I could tell he didn't want to talk about it anymore. I understood that. When something is taking up so much space in your mind, talking about it out loud makes your head feel like it will explode.

Juan Carlos's expression changed, focusing on the block party crowd.

"Hey," he said. "Isn't that Fatima?"

Kareem and I looked. Juan Carlos was right. Fatima was threading her way through the crowd, head swiveling. She was looking for something—or someone.

"FATIMA!" Juan Carlos shouted.

We watched her looking around, trying to find us. When she finally saw us, she nodded and walked toward us in a direct line.

"Good, you're still here," she said. "I was looking for you."

"What are you doing here?" I asked. "I thought you had plans today."

"Today is my sister's birthday party and I was helping put together decorations," she said. "I thought my mom would make me stay for the party, but she seemed to realize that hanging out at a three-year-old's party wouldn't be very much fun for me."

I laughed. "Yeah, the block party is way better."

"You should have an elote," Juan Carlos said. "Have you had them before?"

"I love those!" she smiled. "But later. For now, we need to focus on your communication device. I had a thought and I wanted to see if you'd tried it."

I fought down the defensive feeling that cropped up in me. Why did I always feel defensive when it came to Fatima? It was like the possibility of her having an idea that I hadn't thought of felt like a threat. But, I reminded myself, the goal was to talk to Cheese.

"I've tried a lot of stuff," I said slowly. "What's your idea?"

"Well, maybe the power source needs a power source, if that makes sense. Like a battery is a power source, but only if it's charged, you know? You said it turned on, but maybe it's in stasis or something until it has the energy it needs. Like low power mode or something."

"Yeah, when Cheese was here we figured out that his ship needed light and water to grow the light-flowers," Kareem said. "But it seemed like once the flower was grown, it didn't need anything else. To, you know, sustain it."

Fatima's forehead crinkled.

"Hmm, okay. I guess I need to know more about how it all works. Can I see the light-flower again?"

"I didn't bring it with me," I said. "It seemed too risky. I only took it out of the house the other day at Gadget Beach so you could see proof."

"Gadget Beach?"

I felt myself blush. "Um, the creek where we met you. We call it Gadget Beach. I used to get stuff there to help build inventions and things."

"Cool," she said. "But okay, you don't have it with you. Can we go to your house?"

Again, I felt defensive, but in a different way this time. The idea of Fatima at my house felt weird. I wasn't even sure if I liked her! But I guess some things needed to happen in the name of science.

"Um, okay," I said. "I need to text my mom."

Part of me hoped my mom would tell me no, that I needed to stay at the block party with her and the rest of the family.

Mom: *You're walking with Juan Carlos and Kareem right?*

Me: *Yeah I'm not going by myself.*

Mom: *Okay. That's fine then.*

I sighed.

"Okay," I said. "Let's go."

We filled Fatima in on all the details about Cheese we could think of as we walked. The summer had been such a blur that some things were fuzzy. But we told her about the process of learning how the Pinball ship worked and how we communicated with Cheese. We told her about how Cheese had six eyes and a silver arm. I kept expecting Fatima to be shocked or disbelieving, but she just listened to everything with the same studious face.

By the time we got to my room, I felt like she knew everything there was to know about Cheese and the light-flowers.

"Hold on," I said as we got to the top of the stairs. I left Fatima and Juan Carlos and Kareem outside the door and slipped in by myself first. I rushed around, cleaning things up, stuffing them in the closet and behind Nugget's cage. It wasn't that I cared what Fatima thought, but I bet her laboratory where she got her patents or whatever was a lot more organized than my room.

"Okay," I said, swinging the door open.

We all sat on the floor with the light-flower glowing at the center. Nugget squeaked softly in his cage, but I ignored him for now.

"It does seem to be glowing just fine," she said. "I don't know how long the battery life is for these things, but you'd think it would be dim and wilted if it was running out. So that can't be the issue."

"It has to be something Cheese thought of already," Kareem said. "Cheese wouldn't have left you with a busted device."

"Maybe Cheese knew it was broken and wanted you to fix it," Juan Carlos suggested. "Maybe Cheese is going to swing back around and pick it up."

My chest squeezed at the idea of seeing my friend again. Maybe so.

"I just don't know," I said, shaking my head.

My phone beeped and I reached for it, let my face ID unlock it, and then read the text from my mom.

Mom: *Did you make it back okay?*

I texted her back quickly.

Me: *Yep, I'm home.*

"Wait a minute," Fatima said. "What did you just do?"

"I texted my mom," I said slowly.

"No, when you picked up your phone," she said.

"I . . . looked at it? I unlocked it."

"Face ID," she said.

"Yeah. I set it up the night I got it."

"What if the flower phone has something like that?" she said, looking excited. "Like a passcode?"

"I mean, if it's face ID, I've looked at it a thousand times," I said doubtfully. "From a thousand different angles."

"But what if it's not face ID," Juan Carlos said. "What if there's another way to unlock it? You know, some people use fingerprint unlock for their phones."

We all leaned in, examining every inch of the flower phone again, and I tried placing my finger on a variety of spots, waiting for something to beep or glow or something. Anything. But there was nothing.

I felt disappointment lurking, but Fatima looked more excited.

"I think we're onto something," she said. "What other kinds of passcodes are there?"

"A secret handshake," Kareem joked. He gave the flower device a tap.

"Or Morse code," Juan Carlos said.

"What about a voice key," Fatima said. "Have you tried talking to it?"

"Talking to it?" I repeated, shaking my head. "No, why would I talk to something that can't answer back?"

"You talk to Nugget," Juan Carlos said with a shrug.

I shot him a dirty look.

Fatima didn't bother to ask who Nugget was. She was on the trail of something.

"Try talking to it," she said. "I don't think Morse code would be something an alien from another galaxy would rely on for a key."

"And say what?" I said, feeling silly. "Tell it jokes? Say, 'Open sesame'?"

"Sure," she said, dead serious. "Why not?"

I wished I was alone so I could try this stuff without people looking at me. Mainly without Fatima looking at me. I pick up the light-flower device but I don't know what to say.

"What would you say if you were calling someone?" she said. "It's easy. What do you say when you call your grandma?"

Sometimes simple is the answer, I thought.

"Hi, Cheese," I said, still feeling ridiculous. Nothing happened.

"Maybe hold it a little closer to your face, like how you would talk into a normal phone," Fatima suggested.

I sighed but brought the phone closer to my face. I even spoke louder.

"HI, CHEESE." Still nothing.

We sat there, thinking about what to do next.

"And y'all didn't have a secret code? Or passphrase you used with each other?"

"No," I said, frustrated. "The only thing Cheese even knew how to say was 'Cheese and crackers!'"

What happened next shocked even me.

The light-flower immediately glowed brighter. There was a pulse of fuchsia, and then the smooth gray part of the device shifted, like a mirage in the desert. It went from flat and gray to almost grainy, and then, like magic, an image appeared.

It was Cheese. A recording, it seemed. There Cheese was, waving that metal arm and blinking those six eyes, making all the faces I had come to know meant the alien was happy. Cheese spun around fast, bobbing up and down.

"Cheese and crackers," said a voice I remembered so well. Then there was a light show: Cheese with Cheese's parents and more of Cheese's kind, stars streaking around inside the ship. Wherever Cheese was, our alien friend seemed safe.

Fatima stared with her mouth hanging open. She probably thought we were making it up right until this moment. But I couldn't gloat. I was so happy to see Cheese that I might cry. And actually, I did.

COMMUNICATION IS KEY

Cheese didn't have a problem understanding us, or at least interpreting us. So Juan Carlos and Kareem took turns saying hello and giving updates on their lives. It was amazing that we were able to send Cheese messages. In the reply messages, Cheese was happy to hear from us, bobbing up and down, as Cheese does.

I started every morning by updating Cheese on everything happening on Earth. Well, in Ferrous City at least. "Hey, Cheese! Yesterday in class we learned that the Earth artist Vincent van Gogh painted *The Starry Night* in 1889—and that same year Nintendo was founded as a corporation. They weren't making game consoles yet, but still! Isn't that wild? Some things in history feel like they were a long, long time ago, especially the way they teach them in school sometimes. But they weren't that long ago at all. Is it like that in your world? Do you learn things from teachers, or are you just . . . born knowing stuff? I wish you could tell me everything. Like how this phone works."

Kareem, Juan Carlos, and I—and Fatima, of course—experimented once we figured out that the flower phone was voice-activated. The way to turn it on was to say *cheese and crackers*, the way to start a message was, *Hi Cheese*, and the way to send the message was to say, *send message*. It turned out the flower was powered after all—it just needed voice activation! I marveled at how Cheese managed to program this and leave it for me. Maybe Cheese didn't program it at all. Maybe for an alien it was like snapping your fingers. Or, not your fingers, but . . . something like that. These were all questions I could ask, but I wouldn't ever *really* know the answers.

Cheese understood us, but we didn't understand Cheese.

When I said this to my friends in science class, Kareem and Juan Carlos nodded, looking bummed out. But Fatima shook her head.

"Never say never," she said. "This is what science is all about! Answering questions. There are a lot of unknowns when it comes to your friend. But that doesn't mean we can't make them known. It was only a few decades ago that no one ever walked on the Moon, you know?"

That made me think of what I'd told Cheese about time. Walking on the Moon was a good example. It felt like humans had always been able to go to the Moon, but I'd read enough about Katherine Johnson, the human computer, to know that wasn't true. It took work and time to figure out space travel. Sometimes a lot of time.

"We should probably talk about the actual project," Juan Carlos said seriously. I smiled at our group leader. "I know we can't show them Cheese's phone, but we need to have something more than research. I have an idea."

He hesitated, like we were going to say no. Even though I always wanted to be the leader for projects—especially science—I was getting used to this, and I liked that Juan Carlos was doing it.

"So," he began. "Remember when we first met Cheese? And we were trying to figure out how to talk to an alien? Before we could see the flower movies? Well, I was thinking for the project, we could, you know, show different ways that scientists could try to communicate with aliens if they met them. And it would be like a *what if* for the project but we'd actually be trying them with Cheese. You know?"

My jaw dropped.

"Dude, that's brilliant."

In that instant, Ms. Erivo popped up behind him.

"I don't know what you're working on," she said, grinning. "But based on *brilliant*, it sounds like you all are making good progress!"

"You have no idea," Fatima said.

We did so much work on the project during that class period that my hand still felt like a dinosaur claw after school. But I was glad we did. Fatima's earlier research on NASA communication protocols paid off, and by the time Ms. Erivo's class was over, I felt like I could intern at NASA.

The research showed us steps that alien linguists—people who study language when it comes to aliens—had agreed would be a logical way to communicate with extraterrestrial life. Turns out, numbers are a big part of the plan because math is universal. At least, as far as we know. Some scientists said the best thing to do would be just to list prime numbers. But I only know about eight of them, and, luckily, I think we're beyond that with Cheese. We don't have to prove that there's intelligent life on Earth. He's already been here.

Fatima, Juan Carlos, Kareem, and I discussed this as we made our way to my house.

"If no one minds," Fatima said. "Could I send him a message today? Just based on everything we've talked about?"

I couldn't help it. I still felt a little defensive or maybe possessive when it came to Cheese and Fatima. Luckily, Juan Carlos answered instead.

"Yeah!" he said enthusiastically. "I mean, you're the one who found all those research things about communication. It makes sense."

He was right. *Obviously.* I kept my feelings to myself and tried to remember what Kareem said: *You don't always have to be the smartest.*

I made sure my parents were busy and my brothers were both at their after-school jobs before we went up to my room. I could usually hear someone coming, but every now and then, when I was really focused on something, my family could pop into the room without me hearing them come up, and I didn't want to have to lie even more. Plus, I don't know how I would explain the light-flower.

We all sat down on the floor with the flower phone in the middle.

"Cheese and crackers," I said. We'd figured out that it only responded to my voice to turn on, which gave me a twist of pleasure, honestly.

It immediately powered on and I handed it to Fatima.

"Ready?" I asked. "Do you know what you're going to say?"

"Hi, Cheese," she said, starting to speak right away. "My name is Fatima Adebayo. We've never met, but I wanted to introduce myself. I'm friends with Ethan and we worked together to figure out how to power on your device."

Hearing her say that made me feel guilty for all the negative feelings I have about her. She was nice, and very smart. There was no reason not to like her. And she called me a friend.

"I wanted to tell you that I think it's amazing that you're out there. Wherever you are. I've wondered about it before. Life outside Earth. I mean, the probability of us being the *only* sentient life in the *entire universe* is really low. I wonder how many other planets you've been to. If you have friends across the universe just like us. It's wild to think about."

That sinking feeling was back in my stomach. Why did the idea of Cheese having friends across the universe make me feel sad? I guess I liked the idea of us being special. Of me being special. Either way, there was no way anyone else in the galaxy helped Cheese fix a broken ship and return to the stars while outrunning hunters.

"Anyway, hi," Fatima said. Then she reached for her phone. "And before I say goodbye, I wanted to play you a song. My mom says music is a universal language. So even though you probably don't understand everything I'm saying, maybe you'll understand this."

She tapped PLAY on her phone and the music filled my room. I recognized the words but not the voice. A soft, soothing voice to equally as gentle ukelele. It played while

Fatima smiled and swayed. When the song was finished, Fatima said, "Bye, Cheese. Send message."

The smooth gray part of the device blinked.

"What song was that?" Juan Carlos asked.

"'Somewhere Over the Rainbow' by Israel Kamakaw-iwo'ole," she said. "It just . . . sounds like Earth to me. A friendly Earth."

"Yeah," Kareem said, nodding. "It does. Wow."

I felt like crying. Not in a bad way or even in a sad way. Kind of like in an overwhelmed way.

"But what are lemon drops?" Juan Carlos asked, looking thoughtful.

"They're a type of candy," Fatima said, laughing.

"Oh," he said, patting the flower phone. "Well, that's a friendly Earth, too."

"I wish I knew how it worked," Fatima said, sighing almost dreamily. "Imagine that message shooting across the universe, all the way to wherever Cheese is. Amazing."

"Let's see if a message comes back," Kareem said.

"Cheese always answers," Juan Carlos said. It was true, Cheese always replied within a few minutes. The technology must be powerful, I thought—zapping back and forth the galaxy so fast.

"Look, it's lighting up," Kareem said, excited.

"Listen," I said.

Cheese appeared, spinning and waving and bobbing. I was relieved that Cheese hadn't found some special way to communicate with Fatima, and vice versa. Even if I knew that was petty.

I wondered if Cheese was surprised to see someone new. But if Cheese was worried, there was no sign of it. I liked that an alien trusted us. Cheese knew we would protect the secret, that we'd never do anything to risk its safety.

"I want to send a message, too," Juan Carlos said. He'd only sent one so far.

He took the flower phone and told Cheese all about his parents and what they were going through for the test. Then he decided to play a song, too.

"This is called '*Fotos y Recuerdos*,'" he told Cheese. "By Selena. It's one of my mom's favorite songs." He paused, his face falling. "My parents have lived here for so long. At what point is this just home? Without a test? My abuela says borders are made up. I felt like you wouldn't understand borders, either. This is all just Earth to you, right? Anyway, how are your parents? How is your family? I hope everything is okay with them. I know there's a lot to be afraid of, so let us know. Okay? Send message."

Juan Carlos finished. The device blinked. And the message zipped across the galaxy.

"Have you met Cheese's family?" Fatima asked.

"No," Juan Carlos said. "Just Cheese. But we saw footage of the entire Cheese family. They look a lot alike. There are lots of them. But the aliens hunting them were dangerous and I think Cheese lost a lot of its kind."

We let that settle between us while we waited for Cheese to reply.

"Have you seen any more of that AHA guy?" Fatima asked, looking at me. "Jodie?"

"No," I said. "I sent him on a wild goose chase to the next town. Hopefully, he's still focused on that."

"His parents took him all the way outside the city to hunt aliens?" She laughed. "Wow. My parents wouldn't even drive me to the block party. I had to take the bus."

"If I can't get there by bus, then the place doesn't exist," Kareem said. "Luckily, when we moved, we came back closer to the neighborhood."

My mind jumped to my parents, wondering what decisions they might be making about our move. It wasn't fair that they were figuring it all out in private when it affected me and my brothers, too. Didn't we get a say before it was too late?

"Shouldn't he have written back by now?" Juan Carlos said, interrupting my thoughts. We looked at the flower phone. He was right. Cheese normally would have sent a video by now. We sat waiting, chatting about school and the changes in the neighborhood. But still no message.

"Do you think I said something wrong?" Juan Carlos said, looking worried.

"Definitely not," I said quickly. "He's probably flying to a new planet or something and needs to focus."

After my friends left and I put the flower phone away, it still bugged me in the back of my mind. Cheese always responded. Always.

MR. WHITE...AGAIN

In the morning, there was still no word from Cheese. The seed of worry that had been planted in my stomach last night nestled deeper and had sprouted into a panic by the time I got dressed for school. I wanted to bring the flower phone to school with me, just so I could sneak into the bathroom and check every now and then. Cheese's family was a big worry for Cheese this summer. And now when we asked about them, Cheese went dark.

I barely had any appetite at breakfast, and my dad noticed.

"Ethan, is everything okay?" he said as I stirred my cereal. "You seem like you're out in space."

"Huh?" I said quickly. "What did you say about space?"

He tapped his temple with the end of his spoon.

"I said it seems like your head is floating out there! Is something on your mind?"

"Not really," I said, shrugging. I glanced at him, wondering if this was a time I could get away with pressing a little. "Are we going to live here forever?"

"What do you mean?" He tensed up. I felt guilty asking him questions that I already knew the answers to.

"Like, in this house," I said. "We've lived here forever. And I see a lot of people moving. Are we going to move?"

"Ah," he said, shifting in his seat. "I don't think so. I don't know, Ethan."

"Why are people moving?" I asked.

"For different reasons," he said, sighing. I could tell he wished Mom was there to back him up. Troy paused his sit-ups in the living room to listen. "Some people don't like when the neighborhood changes. Some people think Ferrous City is getting too expensive. Some people need money and houses are going for a lot."

"Do we need money?"

"Everybody needs money," he said.

"Do we—"

"Here's the truth, Ethan," he said. "I'm not prepared for this conversation right now. That's the truth. Let me think about how to best discuss this and we can talk tonight. Okay? Deal?"

"Yeah, sure," I said. I scraped out my cereal bowl and continued getting ready for the day. Silently and separately. When I peeked in at Troy, he hadn't started his sit-ups again. He was just lying on his back staring at the ceiling.

Outside, the air was turning to fall. It was subtle, but it was there. Cool and crisp. I wished Cheese could come and visit and experience another version of Earth. There was no way to describe fall in a video message that would do it justice. Our English teacher had us write poems about the seasons last year, and people read them out loud. The poems were good, but mostly because I knew how fall and winter and spring and summer felt. How could I explain fall so that Cheese could feel it? There had to be a good song out there that made you feel fall when you listened to it. Maybe orchestra music.

"Ethan?"

It was Peter White. Again.

At this point I was ready to sell our house and move just so I didn't have to keep running into the realtor.

"Hi, Mr. White," I said. I kept walking. "I'm on my way to school. Have a nice day."

Mr. White fell into step beside me. "I was just dropping off some paperwork to your neighbor," he said. "What a sweet woman. She told me how sad she would be not to live next to a famous inventor anymore."

"I told you before I'm not famous," I grumbled, embarrassed. "I just like to make stuff."

"You know, I'd be very interested in learning more about the Create Space. What made you decide to choose the factory as a place to host it?"

I felt my cheeks burn. I really am a terrible liar.

"It just seemed convenient," I said, walking faster. "No one was using it, so it made sense."

"Absolutely," he said. "A waste to leave it that way. Seems a little risky, too. An old building like that, away from the public eye. Anything could happen there and no one would know."

"Anything like what?"

"Maybe I've seen too many movies!" he said, laughing. "It just seems like a prime site for trouble. Monsters. Were-wolves. Aliens. That kind of thing."

"Oh," I said. I was starting to sweat. "Well, that kind of thing seems like it would get in the way of inventing stuff. So, uh, glad there's nothing like that around here."

"Thank goodness science fiction stays as fiction," Mr. White said cheerfully. "Although that won't stop the investigators."

"What investigators?"

"Oh, you know, the government. Or conspiracy theorists. I just heard something on the radio the other day about groups coming to Ferrous City to search high and low for alien activity."

"Wh-why?" I said, trying not to sound as nervous as I suddenly felt.

"You know how it is! A rumor starts and it has to be either proven or disproven. Either way, the truth will come out! Have a good day at school, Ethan!"

He turned toward his car, but paused.

"Are you doing okay, Ethan?"

I hesitated.

"Uh, what do you mean?"

"You seem worried. Is something bothering you?"

"Oh, no," I said quickly. "Just . . . you know. Stressed about school. It'll be okay. See ya, Mr. White."

I marched off as quickly as I could before I completely failed at lying.

18

BROTHERLY LOVE

If my head was in the clouds worrying about Cheese, it definitely was now after my conversation with Mr. White. I went back and forth in my head on the way to school, thinking about all the ways this could go wrong. By the time I got to school I felt like I was carrying the weight of the world— and Cheese's world—on my shoulders.

At my locker, I barely looked up when Fatima made a joke about homework. And I just nodded when Kareem and Juan Carlos bantered back and forth over my head. Today was a science block day, but I barely heard a word Ms. Erivo said, even when she told us that she was going to have individual conferences with us to talk about our projects. Usually that would be exciting to me: the chance to talk to my favorite teacher and get her advice on projects and inventions.

"You okay?" Kareem whispered in the middle of class. I could tell Juan Carlos and Fatima were paying attention, too.

"I'm fine," I said. I didn't want them worrying. I had thought that once we got Cheese off-planet he wouldn't be in danger anymore. But Mr. White was right. Jodie was proof enough! Wherever there was a rumor, people were bound to sniff around.

After class, I was ready to slink out the door, but Ms. Erivo called me back.

"Go ahead," she said to Juan Carlos and Kareem, who hung back as if to wait for me. "Ethan will catch up."

They left, casting me concerned looks, and closed the door behind them.

"Is everything alright, Ethan?" Ms. Erivo asked. "You haven't been yourself today."

"I'm okay," I grumbled. "I just have stuff on my mind."

"Anything you think you can share? This is a no-judgment zone."

I shook my head. I wouldn't even know where to begin. In some ways it felt like I hadn't really been the same since Cheese left. Or maybe even since he arrived. But things were definitely weird and not great now.

"Is this about schoolwork? Or something else?" she said.

"There's just a lot going on," I shrugged.

"How about you tell me one thing," she said gently.

"Um . . ."

"Start with *What would you do if . . .*" she suggested. "You don't have to make it about you."

I paused, considering this advice.

"What would you do if . . ." I started. "What would you do if you had to make a choice, but none of the choices seemed like good options?"

"Ah, that is tough," she said. "If no option seems like a good option, and following any path feels wrong, then you have to follow the only thing you can—and that's your gut."

"But shouldn't scientists follow logic?" I asked. "Rationale?"

She laughed. "You think scientists don't have gut feelings? You think scientists always have a reasonable, logical selection of choices to make? No way, Ethan. It's rarely that clean—in science or in life! Sometimes things are messy. And sometimes we have to get messy to do the right thing."

After school I skipped going to my locker and went straight for the exit doors. I didn't want to walk with anyone today. I wanted to walk home alone. Ordinarily, I would go the Create Space after school, but I didn't want to do that, either. I just wanted to be by myself.

At home, the first thing I did was run to my room and check to see if I had a message from Cheese. I almost screamed when I realized that I had left my door slightly open, I'm usually more careful.

I rushed to my room but nothing seemed out of place. The last thing I needed was my mom cleaning up and accidentally throwing away something important.

"Cheese and crackers," I said to activate the communication device. "Hi, Cheese, I just wanted to say, What's up? I'm a little worried since we haven't heard back from you. I know you're probably busy. It's probably silly to worry about you. But still. I have a bad feeling that I can't shake. Let me know that you and your family are okay, alright? Send message."

I sat on the floor of my room and placed Nugget on my lap. He knew I wasn't feeling too great. He didn't even try to chew holes in my shirt as he usually did when he wanted to play. He just sat there and nuzzled me and I petted his back over and over like it was a magic lamp. Even if a genie popped out of my guinea pig, I don't think I'd even know what to wish for. You only get three wishes, and at this point I felt like I had a lot more than three things that needed fixing. Cheese wasn't responding to my messages, my science project wasn't going great, and I didn't know if I could completely trust one of my partners.

I gazed at the flower phone for a minute before pushing it back under my bed. Maybe something was wrong with it. Maybe we had used it too much or something and Cheese only meant it for emergencies. He didn't act like that when he sent us communications, though. Or maybe there was more going on than I could understand.

Downstairs I heard the door slam, which meant Troy was home. He was the only one who ever slammed the door. And I could tell that my parents weren't home because nobody yelled at him.

"Helloooo," he called through the house. I didn't answer. "Ethan, you homeeee?"

I stomped my foot on the floor twice in answer. Maybe that would be enough. But a moment later I could hear him tromping up my stairs.

"Can I come in?" he said through the door. That was different. Usually, he just barged in.

"Yeah."

When he came in, he was smiling, carrying a take-out box from the bodega.

"Look what I got." He grinned, but then he saw my face and Nugget on my lap. His face fell. "Oh no. Did Nugget die?"

"What???"

"You . . . look so sad, and he's just there."

Nugget wiggled and squeaked, looking up at Troy. I can read his little mind: *What? Dude, I'm fine!*

"He's fine," I translated. "He was just letting me pet him while I chilled out."

"So, Nugget is fine," Troy said, coming into the room. He hunkered down on the floor next to me and leaned back against the bed with a big sigh. "But you're not."

"I'm fine," I grumbled.

"You're obviously not," he said.

He held the box out to me. It contained powdered doughnuts from the bodega. I didn't have an appetite, but I reached in anyway. When I took a bite, Nugget was showered with powdered sugar.

"What's on your mind, bro?" Troy said.

The doughnut seemed to loosen my tongue. And, well, he was my brother.

"A lot of stuff, I guess," I said. "Nothing makes sense lately."

"Is this about the girl?" he said. "Di?"

"What? No!" I shook my head angrily. "Not everything is about a girl, you know."

"You're right, my bad. So, what doesn't make sense?"

"Ever since this summer . . ." I trailed off. So many things happened this summer. So many things it's like they won't even all fit inside my head at one. Cheese. The Others. My dad. The cops. "I don't know who to trust."

He slowly set the box on the floor, wiping his hand on his pant leg. Then he shifted and reached to put his arm around my back. I stiffened, and then relaxed.

"It was a bad time," he said. "I think about it every day. Sometimes I'm just walking through the front yard and it hits me, like it's happening again right then. I start sweating."

"Nobody is safe," I said. My chest felt tight. The more we talked, the closer we got to what was bothering me.

I don't know who to trust. I don't know who will keep us safe. I don't know how to protect the people (and creatures) I love. I don't know how anything works.

"We're safe," he said. "When we're together. We're as safe as we can be when we're together and talking and loving each other. And you gotta listen to me when I say that everything you're feeling is normal and okay. But you don't have to feel it alone."

We sat silently like that for a while, Nugget half on my lap and half on Troy's. He licked the traces of powdered sugar off his little claws.

"You can always talk to me about stuff, okay?" he said. "I know things feel different. You're getting older and—"

"Ugh! Don't talk to me about puberty, Troy!"

"I'm not!" he laughed. "I'm just saying your mind is changing. You're noticing stuff little kids don't notice. You're feeling the weight of the world. But you don't have to carry it alone. And the main point is, you *can't*. You have to let people help you."

I nodded silently, the words sinking in. They felt like the tiger balm my dad put on my leg when I got a cramp. I reached for another doughnut and so did he.

"I can't believe you thought Nugget was dead," I muttered.

"Well, his cage kind of smells like it."

I shoved him and he laughed and we ate more doughnuts until we heard our parents come home.

"I'll get rid of the evidence," he said, folding up the box. "But you have to pretend to eat dinner. And Ethan?"

"Yeah?"

"Sometimes you gotta distract yourself," he said. "Get out of your head. Do something you don't usually do. If you don't know what to do or can't figure something out, put your mind elsewhere. It'll come to you."

I nodded as he slid out through the door. I checked to see if Cheese had sent a communication, and when I saw there was nothing new, I followed my brother downstairs.

Mom and Dad had already taken their seats in the living room. As soon as Troy and I came down, Dad put a hand on Mom's knee, like she needed comfort or something. I gulped as I sat down on the couch next to Chris, nose-deep in his phone. The last time they'd been this serious had been the police talk. I found myself mimicking my dad as he took a deep breath before speaking.

"I know you've all seen what's been happening lately with the neighborhood," Dad said. "How the cost of living's been going up."

"Yeah, it's gonna take me an extra six months to afford those Jordans I was eyeing," Chris said.

"Not to mention groceries," Mom added. "The important stuff, too."

Dad cleared his throat. "As you know, your mother has taken the day shift in the last few weeks. It was a decision we made for reasons other than money." He gave Mom a soft look. "She needed to work the day shift for her mental health and I was happy to support her in that decision." He paused. "But my shift manager told me I'm not getting the raise I was banking on to make up the difference."

So this was all real. We did have money trouble and now it had details.

"There are a couple ways to go about this," Dad continued. "We could do a lot of reshuffling—"

"And not at the expense of finishing high school and going off to college," Mom added, looking right at me a moment.

"—But one quick thing to do is do what Mrs. McGee did. Sell the house, move to the closest cheaper area. Troy and Chris's school serves multiple neighborhoods—"

And then it hit me.

"Not mine!" I exclaimed. "We can't move! I can't leave my friends!" The things I'd lose piled up in my brain. "I can't leave the Create Space or—" Or Cheese's landing site. That was the only place Cheese knew; what if he ever wanted to come back?

"Okay, okay, Ethan," Dad said, raising his voice a bit. "We don't have to put that one on top. But reshuffling would mean . . ." He looked to Troy and Chris. "Everyone helping."

Chris shrugged. "I could wait longer on the shoes, give some more cash to the pot."

"I can take on more shifts," Troy said. Mom gave him a dirty look. "And if my grades go down, then I'll stop. But I can contribute more, too."

"And I can get a job, too!" I interjected. I could handle it with all this alien stuff no problem. I thought. "Even just . . . mowing lawns and stuff."

Troy snorted. "You could probably make a fortune fixing appliances, if you still remember how they're supposed to be put together."

I glared at Troy, but he was right. I could do that.

"Alright," Dad said. "We'll start with that. Good talk."

With that, everyone headed their own way. I went back up to my bedroom, trying to process everything about Di and money and Cheese. And Nugget, too.

I double- and triple-checked that Nugget's cage door was shut before I went to bed. My whole family can look out for each other, but I'm the only one really looking out for the little guy.

19

A GOOD DEED

I was determined to make the next day a better day—even when I woke up and found that Cheese still hadn't responded. I sat on my bed, sighed deeply, and then got dressed for my day. I thought about what my brother had said, about not being able to carry the weight of the world alone. I knew he was right. But I didn't know how to go about shifting the weight to anyone else without making things complicated for them. Or for Cheese.

I thought I'd try something different. I decided to take a new route to school. I went out the back door, climbed over the backyard fence, and snaked through the alley between the neighbors' houses. When I got to the main street, I picked up on my usual route to school, trying to figure this whole thing out.

At school, I made my way to my locker and overheard Di talking to her friend Marley by the front desk. "They said if I wanted to ask for more vegetarian options in the cafeteria, then I had to collect at least fifty signatures and deliver the petition to the lunch staff. But I'm always doing petitions, you know? I feel like no one is going to take me seriously anymore if I care about *everything*."

I thought about what my brother said about getting outside my head and doing something different. When I got to my locker, I grabbed one of the big blank pieces of paper I kept stashed in there for sketching inventions. And when I got to homeroom, I laid it out on the table, writing carefully. Kareem was in a different homeroom, but Juan Carlos was in mine. When he arrived, he leaned over my shoulder.

"What are you doing?" Juan Carlos paused and read what I was writing. "Oh, cool. Can I sign?"

"Of course."

Over the course of the morning, I got lots of other people to sign, too, including my teachers. By lunchtime, I had a page of signatures—fifty-two names. I waited until I saw Di enter the cafeteria before I went to the lunch line.

"Here you go, Ms. Walden," I said to the head lunch lady. She peered down at the big piece of paper I handed her. Di entered the line a second later.

"We, the students of Ferrous City Elementary, express our support for including more vegetarian options on the daily school lunch menu," she read out loud.

"What is this?" Di said, walking up. "Who did this petition?"

She turned her eyes to me.

"Did you do this?" she said.

I nodded, suddenly embarrassed. But then her face lit up in a smile and the tightness in my chest melted away. Ms. Walden thanked me for the petition and said she would discuss it with the principal. Di followed me to the lunch table, where we both sat down with lunch from home.

"You're not even a vegetarian!" she said. "That's really cool."

"It seems ridiculous that there aren't more options," I said. "A growing percentage of kids identify as vegetarian. And some people don't eat meat because of their religious beliefs and stuff."

She smiled and I did, too, but I was glad when Kareem and Juan Carlos showed up a second later. Fatima was right behind them and she slid in next to Di.

"So," Fatima said, leaning across the table. "Can I send a message to Cheese today? I watched this movie called *Arrival*. It's about this scientist who is learning to communicate with aliens, and it made me think of ideas. I want to try something with Cheese and . . ."

"Wait, wait, wait," Di interrupted, her voice in a hiss. "You know about Cheese?"

Fatima stopped, looking back and forth between us all.

"I do now, yeah. I've been helping Ethan, Juan Carlos, and Kareem with a project. I only brought it up because they said you were there this summer, too."

"Yeah, I was," Di said, shooting me a curious look. I could tell she was asking *Are you sure we can trust this girl?*

"She's cool," I said, nodding. "She won't tell anybody."

Di relaxed.

"Okay," she said. "But we probably shouldn't talk about it at school, right? At least not in here. You never know who's listening."

We went out the back door after school. I was surprised that Di met us there, too. She was usually busy with all her clubs and activities. But, together with her, the five of us meandered back to my house, where I went upstairs and got the light-flower.

"Let's go back to Gadget Beach," Fatima said. "I didn't get a chance to explore it the last time I was there."

We all agreed and we made our way there. They all seemed so casual as they walked. I couldn't help but feel the weight of my worries about Cheese pressing down on me. Mr. White said he heard something on the radio about aliens in Ferrous City. And the goo-intruder knew where I lived. Have I been keeping my head in the sand? I suddenly felt irresponsible for taking the light-flower out of my house. But, then again, if someone was trying to track down alien stuff, I'd rather they come to Gadget Beach than my house. The idea of the cops messing with my family again made me feel shaky.

"Penny for your thoughts," Di said. "Dime for your mind."

I forced a laugh. "Nobody would even give chewed gum for my thoughts."

Down at Gadget Beach, everything was as it usually was. The creek trickled along and the junk was piled high all around.

"Okay," Fatima said, sitting down on a stack of tires. "Let's do this."

I took the light-flower phone out of my backpack and said, "Cheese and crackers." Then I handed it to Fatima.

Before she began to speak, she unzipped her backpack and pulled out squares of posterboard. She'd cut them up into smaller squares, the size of my hand. Each one was a different color.

"Hey, Cheese," she said. "It's Fatima again. I've been thinking that if you're able to send us a message soon, we could practice learning some of your language. I have some tools that I've learned. I'm not an expert. But maybe you can tell us how to say the names of colors." She paused, then picked up the pieces of posterboard one at a time. "This is red. This is orange. This is blue. And this is purple. How do you say these? In your language? Send message."

The message was sent and we sat on Gadget Beach silently for a minute.

"I hope Cheese is okay," I said quietly.

"Try not to be too worried, Ethan," said Juan Carlos. "Who knows what kind of busy alien life Cheese lives. Like, we can't understand, so we don't know if Cheese has school and stuff, too. Cheese might have a big project due! A project, like, studying humans!"

We all laughed at that, even me. At least until I realized that Juan Carlos was telling me not to worry when I hadn't even told him I was worried. My face had been telling things I didn't mean to tell.

"Hey, I think he wrote back!" Fatima said. I jerked to attention. We'd noticed the fuchsia flicker that happened before, quick as a blink. I grabbed the light-flower phone and played the video.

There was Cheese, swaying back and forth on the device. The image was hazy, like the connection wasn't as strong as it had been. A silver arm waved. Six eyes blinked at us. Cheese twirled.

"That looks far away," Juan Carlos said. "See, Ethan, Cheese was traveling and that's why we haven't heard back!"

I watched Cheese and I felt the usual affection that I always felt when I saw my friend. But something was off. Cheese seemed sad. Or sick. I couldn't put my finger on it. It was just *different*.

"I've been watching how Cheese moves as part of my communication study," Fatima said. "This is new. See that sway? That's new. I wonder what Cheese is trying to tell us."

Cheese twirled again, which I knew meant he was happy. But the twirl was jerky.

"I wonder how far away Cheese travels," said Kareem. "What would that be like? To just go as far into the stars as they'll take you."

"I'll be right back," I said, standing up. "I'm going to run up the hill to the Create Space and use the bathroom." I turned away quickly in case my face was giving away something I didn't want it to. I climbed the trench out of Gadget Beach. I didn't want to go all the way to the Create Space, but I did need a minute alone. I cut across the field, walking slowly.

I made it halfway across the grass when Jodie appeared.

20

BWH

"Whoa," I said, surprised. "What are you doing here?"

He looked like his feelings were hurt.

"I don't need permission to walk around in this field, *Ethan*," he said defensively.

"No, I know. I just . . ."

"I'm looking for evidence, if you must know," Jodie he said. He held a bundle of plants. "I keep seeing chatter that says there was alien activity around the old factory where you made the Create Space. I'm not giving up until I find proof and deliver it to the BWH."

"The what?"

"You've never heard of the BWH?"

"No, Jodie."

"The BWH," he said matter-of-factly. "The Bureau for Weird Happenings."

"Um, that sounds made up," I said.

"Some people say it is," he said, shrugging. "But I think it's real. And I wouldn't be surprised if they showed up soon. I saw chatter today that says a BWH investigative unit is on their way here *right now*."

"Why would you say that?" I said, feeling my temper rising. "Why would they?"

He looked as surprised as I did when I first ran into him.

"Why would they? You mean why wouldn't they! You've seen the old movies, right? *E.T.* and stuff? They want to meet aliens and do experiments on them. Or figure out what kind of technology they have so we can use it, too. You know. *Science.*"

"That doesn't sound like science," I said. I could hear my voice getting louder but I couldn't stop it or quiet down. "That sounds like—I don't know—kidnapping! Stealing!"

"Um, whoa," Jodie said, with his hands (and plants) held up. "I don't know why you're getting so mad."

"Because you're trying to track down something that . . ." I finally stopped myself before I gave anything away. "Something that doesn't even exist."

"They do exist! And we need to be ahead of them if they're going to attack—"

There it was. People always assume the worst in things they don't understand. Cheese would never attack anyone! In fact, only one sentient life-form here seems set on violence.

"And even if aliens do exist, you want to hurt them!? Stay away from the Create Space. What you're doing isn't science."

I stormed off, going toward the highest grass of the field. I wove through it, zigzagging in the direction of Gadget Beach, my pulse pounding in my ears. I was so angry I couldn't see straight, marching through the trees at the edge of the field. I pushed on, not slowing down even when I could hear the voices of my friends, laughing and talking. I started running, then ran all the way to the slope that led down to Gadget Beach. Then I hurtled forward, sliding and skidding down the little hill until I toppled forward, rolling in the dirt.

I could have lain there forever, but four pairs of hands pulled me to my feet, grabbing me and dusting me off and checking me for cuts.

"Ethan! Ethan, are you okay? What happened?"

I couldn't catch my breath. I was crying. Hard. Not tears. Heavy sobs that vibrated up from my throat. All the weight I'd been carrying on my own finally came crashing down.

"Ethan," Kareem said. He put his hands on my shoulders and looked me in the eye. "Everything is okay. You're okay."

My brother's words echoed in my mind—that we're safe when we're together—which made me want to cry more. Maybe we were safe, but Cheese wasn't. And keeping all these secrets from my family had already gotten my dad roughed up by police. What else could happen? To him? To us?

"I'm not . . . I'm not . . ." I stammered. I still couldn't catch my breath.

Fatima wrapped her arms around me. "Ethan," she said loudly, with authority. "You have to breathe. *Breathe.*"

Maybe it was because I was so surprised, or maybe it was her boss voice. But I did. I breathed, and breathed, until I could breathe regularly again. Everyone was staring at me with concern. It made me want to stand up and run away all over again. But I couldn't. I had to stay.

"Guys," I said. "I think we've got trouble."

THREATS FROM PESTS

After I told them about Mr. White's feeling that investigations would be happening soon and Jodie hearing about the BWH, everyone was silent. I could almost hear the flowers growing. I watched their expressions change from confusion to understanding to disappointment to fear.

"I wish you hadn't kept this a secret," Juan Carlos said, breaking the silence. "We could have been figuring it out together. And because you kept it a secret, now things could get worse."

"I know," I said. "I know. I'm sorry."

Juan Carlos's eyes filled with tears.

"You think you're worried," he said. "So am I. My parents. This test. They've been worried about the citizenship test for so long. What if the BWH or whoever figures out that we were involved with the aliens? What if we get in trouble? What if I mess up my parents' chance?"

"We don't know—" I started, but Juan Carlos interrupted me.

"Exactly, we don't know," he said. "They wouldn't be doing all this if they didn't want to get their hands on an alien. They never just want information. They'll do whatever it takes to get it. I know how this stuff goes."

The look on his face made me want to crumple up in a ball.

"Jodie could be wrong," I said. "He could just be seeing nonsense. You know people say anything on social media."

"Do you know how hard it is for families like mine to stay together?" Juan Carlos said quietly. "Do you know how hard it is to come to a new country, especially a country like this, and start over? It's like there are all these forces trying to tear us apart, and we're fighting so hard to stay together. And now there's another thing trying to tear us apart. And I didn't even know about it. And now it might be too late."

"I'm so sorry," I said, hanging my head. "I just didn't want anyone to worry."

"You can't figure everything out on your own, Ethan," Kareem said, looking at the ground. "You have to trust other people to help sometimes."

"I know," I said. "I'm starting to realize that."

Di and Fatima had been quiet up until now, but now Di spoke up.

"Okay," she said. "Honestly, not that this doesn't matter, cuz it does. But we need to figure out what we're going to do. Like now. Pronto."

"She's right," Fatima said. "And I think the first step in this solution is telling Cheese that we can't communicate anymore."

"What?" I cried.

"Not forever," she said. "But for now. We can't give the Bureau of Weird Happenings, or whatever it's called, any reason to suspect us. They can only have something on us if we have something to give them. And if we're not talking to Cheese, then they've got nothing."

"She's right," Kareem said. "We have to pretend everything is normal and there are no aliens around. Maybe it will blow over and they'll go to another town."

"Fine," I said, struggling to push my anger and sadness down. I knew they were right. But it felt like burning the bridge that I was standing on. Cheese was my friend. And I couldn't shake the fear that there was something to worry about. What if Cheese needed me? And I couldn't talk? What if the alien reached out for help and I couldn't respond without making things even worse? *No good options.*

"Do you want to tell him, Ethan?" Fatima said, extending the flower phone.

"Yes," I said.

I took the device in both hands and stared down at it for a minute before saying, "Cheese and crackers." The device started to glow. I took a deep breath. Man, this felt bad.

"It's Ethan," I said, trying to keep my voice from shaking. "I've got some bad news, buddy. There's an agent on our tail who says that he's tracking you. He claims that aliens are dangerous and he's trying to keep everyone safe, but I know better than to believe that, okay? I don't think you're dangerous. I know you're our friend. So, I don't want you to think that we think you're a villain. We know you're not. But we need to stop talking for a while. I'm so sorry, but this is for the best. If we cut off communication, the agents will have nothing to track, and maybe they'll go away and leave all of us alone. We're doing this to keep you safe. And, you know, to keep us safe, too. Okay? Can you let us know you got this? We'll be thinking about you all the time, buddy. Send message."

"Should we pick a song to play?" Fatima asked. "To help him understand?"

"I think he'll understand well enough," Di said quietly. She put her hand on my back as I swallow back my tears. It was never supposed to be like this. How could things go so wrong?

"It's for the best," Kareem said. "And, like Fatima said, it's not forever."

"Yeah," I said. I tried to imagine a future where talking to Cheese was like talking to Kareem or Juan Carlos. I tried to imagine taking a call in front of my parents, like it was no big deal. Why did it have to be a big deal? Earth made things so complicated.

"Cheese sent a message back," Fatima said quietly. I looked down at the tiny pink glow.

I held it up so we could all see. There was Cheese—acting strangely. The swaying motion was worse, and when Cheese spun, it was clumsy and unnatural.

"This looks weird," Juan Carlos said. "I can't put my finger on it. It reminds me of something."

Cheese waved a silver arm, and I remembered how we used to fist-pump. The way Cheese moved had changed, like Cheese was inside his body for the first time and figuring out how all the parts worked.

"Is Cheese okay?" Fatima whispered to herself.

"Should we send another message, real quick?" Di said. "And ask what's going on? Or should we just assume this means message received?"

"I don't know," I replied, studying Cheese's movements. "Usually, Cheese would do things to communicate, but this message is like sending a blank card. It doesn't say anything, you know?"

"Maybe this is a new part of alien communication," Fatima said, frowning. "Maybe it's something we haven't seen before because Cheese is trying to tell us something different."

"I don't think so," Di said. "Cheese looks weird. Like a puppet."

"Wait," Juan Carlos cried. "Did you see that?"

"What?" I said, leaning in.

"Watch the eyes," Juan Carlos said. "It's like they slip."

Sure enough, it looked as though there was a film over Cheese that shifted, blurring the eyes.

"It's like a photo filter," Di said. "When the phone glitches or you move too fast."

"Weird," Juan Carlos said. "Wait, we have another message!"

I scrambled to open it, and there was Cheese again, still swaying. The alien spun more than the last video, like Cheese was trying hard to show happiness. But now that I had noticed what Juan Carlos pointed out, I watched the eyes blur over and over again. My stomach knotted.

"Something's happening," Kareem said in a tense voice. "Look."

Cheese's message sped up, like it was on fast-forward. The blurring around the eyes spread to the body. Cheese twitched and swayed, faster and faster.

"Oh no," Di said. "It's—"

I realized it just as she did. My hands shot out and grabbed Kareem and Juan Carlos, squeezing them as the realization spread through me. The film over Cheese was slipping away. The blurring spread and the swaying suddenly made sense. The movements smoothed out, serpentine and almost graceful. The six eyes were replaced with three. The shape of Cheese's body began to morph.

It was no longer Cheese.

It was a light-thief, staring straight at us.

22

WHAT IN THE!? NOT ANOTHER ONE!

"Wh-what is that?" Fatima stammered.

"That's a light-thief," Di said grimly, staring at the serpentine face on the communication device without blinking. I knew exactly what was happening in her head because it was the same thing happening in mine: playing back the memories of this past summer, everything the light-thieves put Cheese through, and what we managed to escape from. And now here one was, pretending to be Cheese.

"Have we been talking to a light-thief the whole time?" Juan Carlos said, his chin trembling slightly. "Were we ever talking to Cheese?"

"We had to have been at first," I insisted. "He knew too much about us and stuff that we all did together. Unless—"

"Unless he has Cheese captive," Di said, her eyes huge. "Do you think that's possible? Is Cheese a prisoner?"

"We have no way of knowing," I said.

"Can someone please tell me what a light-thief is?" Fatima cried. "Is that a monster?"

"Pretty much," Kareem said. "They're aliens, too, but they're not like Cheese. The light-thieves steal and destroy. Cheese's people cultivate the light-flowers, and the light-thieves . . . well, it's obvious. They steal the power and exploit it."

"How was it able to look like Cheese?"

"They can change their appearance," I said, shaking my head. "They're horrible. And now we know that they're not done with Earth."

"But what do they want?" Fatima said. "With us? With Cheese?"

"I don't know," Juan Carlos said. "But I have a feeling we're about to find out. Look."

There was another message on the flower phone. My stomach had turned into a ball of steel. We opened the message. The light-thief's face stared at us, its lips twitching. I couldn't breathe. I don't know what I expected, but every time it blinked, my muscles twitched, like my body was ready to run away without me. We stared at it silently, waiting.

Finally, it spoke. One word. In a voice that sounded like oil.

"Earth."

Then the light-thief smiled a vicious, twisted smile and the video ended, leaving me and my friends staring at the flower phone, our hearts pounding.

"What's going to happen?" Juan Carlos said. "What does it want?"

"I don't know, but this seems bad," Kareem said.

For once, Fatima didn't say anything. She looked like she'd been struck by lightning. That's how I felt, too. Like my whole body was electrified but I couldn't move.

"I don't know, either," I said. "And we have no way of reaching Cheese."

The truth was crushing me. The worry for my family, the worry for Cheese's family, the worry for my neighborhood, and now the worry for my entire planet. Because we knew what light-thieves were capable of. From Cheese's people they stole power. *What are they planning to do to us?*

"It said Earth," Di said, like she was reading my mind.

I nodded.

"Maybe they're coming for revenge," Kareem said. "We took a couple of them out, after all."

"Whatever it is," Fatima said, her voice shaking. "It can't be good. Did you see that smile?"

"Whatever they want," Di cried. "We have to be ready to stop them, to fight back—"

"How!?" Juan Carlos asked. "We were able to stop them over the summer, but there were only two of them! We got super lucky!"

My anger grew and grew. I grabbed the light-flower phone. I held it up, activated it, and prepared to send another message. This time I knew who would be listening.

"Hey, you," I said when the recording began. "We don't know what you want, but we know who you are and what you've done. You're not welcome here. If you come for us, we will stop you. Send message."

"Good message," Kareem said quietly. "But how are we ever going to back it up?"

"I don't know," I said. "We'll think of something."

"They'll send scouts first," Fatima said. She was still staring at the flower phone, but she had a sharper look in her eyes. Now that I knew her a little better, I could tell when her gears were turning. She was trying to find a solution, and for once I wasn't feeling jealous or competitive about it. "Like, that creature has been pretending to be Cheese, why?"

"To keep Cheese from telling us something important," Kareem said.

"Bingo," I agreed.

"Yes, and to spy. To get information and see what we know," Fatima added.

"Yeah," I said. "That makes sense. A scout's been lurking around picking up information. And if the scout is already here—that means there are more on the way."

"Maybe our device was modified," Fatima said. I realized now she was kind of talking to herself. I wondered if this was how she worked in her lab or her room or whatever. Thinking out loud, crunching through solutions.

"How would a light-thief modify the light-flower phone?" Di said, frowning. "Without us noticing?"

"I have no idea," I said, my heartbeat slamming inside me. "I took it outside twice. Today and the other time. Unless . . ."

"Do you think it went into your house?" Kareem said, his eyes huge. "The light-thief?"

"That's exactly what happened," I said, hanging my head. I couldn't keep my secret anymore. I had to tell my friends.

"The day before the block party there was an intruder in my house. I think it was the light-thief."

"What!? Why didn't you tell us?" Kareem asked.

That was a good question. I was always trying to solve things by myself, and this was no different. I was starting to realize that maybe I don't have to work through my problems all alone.

"I don't know, I guess I didn't want to say anything until I had all the answers. I'm sorry y'all. Now the light-flower phone is contaminated."

As usual, Fatima was a step ahead of me. She snatched the light-flower phone out of my hands and turned it over and over, lightning fast.

"Fatima, what are you—?"

She reached into the big pockets of her cargo pants and whipped out a palm-sized kit containing what looked like three tiny screwdrivers. Without saying a word, she gripped the screwdriver like a knife. I realized what she was about to do too late.

"Wait!" I cried.

But the sparks were already flying. A quick burst of yellow.

"Oh, no," Juan Carlos yelped. "What did you do?!"

"I found the modifier," she said. She held it up. "And removed it."

It looked like a grain of rice. But the hole in the light-flower phone was bigger.

"I noticed this little thing the other day, and I thought I was tripping because it wasn't on the original sketch I made. But it's so tiny I just thought I missed it. I should have known better."

"I can't believe this," I said, my breathing shallow.

"So the light-thief *snuck into your house* and put that modifier on there," Di said. "And then, what? Intercepted all our videos to Cheese?"

"Now we can't reach Cheese at all," Juan Carlos said, staring at the damage on the flower phone that was caused by removing the modifier. My stomach sank even deeper at the sight of a tiny plume of smoke rising from the phone.

"Fatima did what she had to do," I said firmly. "We don't know if the light-thief scout could track the modifier or not."

"I'm assuming so," Di said. "That kind of seems like basic alien technology."

"Agreed," I said. "So, thank you, Fatima, for finding and removing the problem so fast."

She smiled a weak smile.

"But now we need to figure out how we're going to be able to contact Cheese," Kareem said. "Cheese is probably wondering why we haven't communicated in so long."

"And maybe Cheese can tell us what to do," Juan Carlos said. "Some advice, you know?"

"But how are we going to do all that?" Kareem said, poking the smoking flower phone with his index finger. "This is, uh, not a great place to start."

"We can fix it," I said confidently. "Fatima is smart. I'm smart. We're *all* smart. This is a group project right? We're going to fix it."

"You have a plan?" Kareem said, looking doubtful.

"I mean, no, not exactly," I said. The pressure felt intense—figuring everything out, always having to have the solution. I realized suddenly that I put a lot of that pressure on myself.

"Fatima," I said. "What do you think?"

She looked surprised, staring at me with the device still smoking in her hands.

"You're right, Ethan. We can fix it," she said, determined. "Let's do it."

23

WILL THE REAL CHEESE PLEASE
STAND UP!?

"What else do you have in those pockets, girl?" Di said, nodding at Fatima's cargo pants.

We all kind of laughed.

"Actually . . ." Fatima reached down into the left pocket.

"What is *that*?" Kareem asked.

"It's a pocket soldering iron," she said. "You never know when you'll need it."

I raised my eyebrows, impressed. *This is why she had two patents. Dang.*

"The only thing is," she said, looking concerned. "What do we patch the hole with? It's not like we can just slap glue over the hole and call it a day, you know?"

"We don't have glue anyway," Kareem muttered.

"Actually . . ." I said, reaching toward my backpack. "Teamwork." I smiled and looked at Fatima.

"Well, okay, then," Di said, laughing.

"We have the tools," Fatima said. "But I still don't know how we're going to fix it. Tools aren't enough. We need material. We need to be able to find something that fits, maybe even several somethings."

She trailed off, looking frustrated. I was, too, but only for a minute.

I laughed out loud.

"It's not funny, Ethan," Di said in a low voice.

"No, no, I know!" I said. I threw my arms out. "But look around. Guys! We're at Gadget Beach! If we're going to find something to help fix Cheese's phone, it's going to be here! Right? I've found *everything* here for my inventions. I'll bet anything that we can find something here that we can use to fix the device."

"So, this is *your* lab," Fatima said with a smile, and I grinned.

"Something like that."

It felt good not to have all the answers. This must have been what my brother meant about not carrying the weight of the world on my shoulders. When you spread the weight around, you felt like you could move. It made problems feel smaller. Even when they were still huge.

"Okay," I said. "Let's spread out. Grab anything you think could work. Not just hunks of metal, right, Fatima? But stuff that could be wired? Are there wires?"

Fatima pulled yet another tool out of one of her pockets—a magnifier—and studied the hole in Cheese's phone even more closely.

"There are some simple wirings," she said. "Luckily the modifier didn't get deep into the brain of this device. I don't think I could fix that. But this is basically, like, patching a cut. Getting the wires back together like a scab."

"Okay," I said. "So, wires. Stuff that can be used to patch. Nothing plastic. Metal and wires. Got it?"

Everybody nodded, and without saying anything else, we started scanning Gadget Beach. I hadn't done this in a long time. We'd been so busy at the Create Space that I hadn't had time. Plus being focused on school. Right away I remembered why this was one of my favorite places. I sifted through old computers and keyboards and computer mice. Whenever I glanced at one of my friends, they were unspooling big cables, or digging other unidentifiable junk out of the grit. That was the great thing about us being different. We each had a different eye, and what I would think to dig up is different than what Juan Carlos would.

When we got back together again, we had a big collection of seemingly random stuff. We dumped it all into a pile. Fatima plopped down and began sifting through the goods, examining each piece and casting it aside. While we'd been sweeping the beach, she had been setting up a little workspace where she had the flower phone laid out in a patch of sun. Now she just needed to find something that would work.

I felt a little useless just sitting and watching. But that's exactly what the four of us did while Fatima experimented. It seemed like nothing would work. The "reject" pile got bigger and bigger as our hope diminished.

But then Fatima used her screwdriver to open the back of an old handheld video game console and her eyes brightened.

"This just might work," she said, and turned quickly to the workspace where the flower phone waited.

We watched as she used a pair of tiny clippers to remove wires from the back of the Switch as well as a minuscule ring of copper. Then she used her pocket soldering iron to melt the edges. She did it so carefully and so confidently, it was like watching a surgeon. She really does know her physics.

"I just have to be careful not to melt the flower phone materials," she said to herself. "They look really delicate."

I had never soldered anything. I held my breath while she did the careful work. When she was done, it looked exactly like what she had planned to make: a patch. There was damage to the device, but Fatima had gone in and connected the wires one by one, and then smoothed it over with the copper.

"What do you think?" she said quietly. "Should we try it?"

"Do you think it will work?" Juan Carlos asked.

"Only one way to find out," I said. I took a deep breath, leaned over the flower phone and said as clearly as I could: "Cheese and crackers."

There was a long pause. It felt too long. Way too long. But then . . .

"Oh my gosh," Di said.

"I think it's working," Kareem breathed.

I was too nervous to speak. I held my breath as the flower phone flickered to life. The fuchsia glow was dim at first and then stronger, as if it was drinking up the power from the light-flower now that Fatima had fixed its connection.

And then Cheese's image flowed out of the device.

"Cheese and crackers," Cheese said, waving a silver arm. It was really Cheese. There was no more eye film, no more strange movements.

"Cheese! Thank goodness you're okay! The light-thieves, they hacked our phone!"

Juan Carlos was drawing furiously on the back of one of Fatima's posterboards. He held it up a second later. A rudimentary drawing of a light-thief.

"Send message."

A response came in seconds later. Cheese's body was still and rigid as the image faded and a memory video played.

In the footage, there were the light-thieves, scaly and slithering and baring their terrible teeth as they chased

Cheese's people across the fields of light-flowers. Both flowers and Cheese's people fell. It was horrible. Later in the memory, they fought back. Fire leapt in a wall across the field, moving after the light-thieves like the wave of a slow hurricane. And the light-thieves ran away, fleeing the planet back to their ships.

"Fire?" Di said aloud. "They don't like fire?"

As Cheese's video continued, we saw a cold swampy place. Slimy and green and dank-looking.

"That must be where the light-thieves are from," Kareem said. "They definitely wouldn't be used to fire."

As the images of the fire and the swamp faded away, my friend looked very scared. Cheese's six eyes were big and worried. Those eyes had seen what the light-thieves were capable of firsthand. Cheese had lost many of its kind. I didn't want that to happen again. There or here.

"Be. Careful," Cheese said. I was so shocked by his speaking English—even heavily accented with his alien voice—I didn't blink the entire time I recorded our reply.

"We will be careful, Cheese. You, too! Where are you now? Send message."

We stood there silently for a moment, but we didn't get a response. The reality began sinking in.

"Well," Fatima said. "We don't have time to wait for backup. We need to make our moves."

"Agreed," Di said.

"We need to prepare defenses," Kareem said. We all looked at him.

"Like, flame flowers," Juan Carlos said.

"Okay, let's, um, think about that," I said. "But Fatima is right. We need to move fast. Let's buddy up and start working. Kareem, you and Juan Carlos go with Fatima. Di, do you want to come with me?"

She nodded. I felt my confidence build.

"Let's do it."

24

BE HELPFUL, NOT CREEPY

We raced from Gadget Beach through the field and back to the streets, agreeing to meet at Hathaway Park in one hour.

"Remember," I said. "Avoid people you don't know. Don't talk to anybody unnecessarily. And if you see a tall White guy who looks like he was in the military, go the other direction. We need to avoid all adults—the light-thief scout could look like anyone. Especially that real estate guy, Mr. White. Something tells me he isn't who he says he is."

Everyone nodded, and even though we were all scared, I could tell that we all felt the same determination. If we all worked together to fix Cheese's device, then who says we can't work together to stop an alien species that wants to terraform our planet?

Di and I dashed down the street, cutting corners and taking alleyways. It felt strange to be alone with her, even if we weren't really *alone* as we weaved through groups of people walking down the sidewalks. We'd only ever been at school, or at the Create Space, or killing evil aliens at the factory before the Create Space ever existed. I didn't know when things started to feel different, but as we made our way back to my house, I was very aware that they were.

"Ethan, hold up," Di said, skidding to a stop.

"What's up?"

"Look over my shoulder. You see that black car?"

I glanced up, trying not to be obvious. I saw it. A black car with black windows, cruising slowly about fifty feet behind us. I darted my eyes at Di and nodded.

"I saw it on the last block, too," she said, sounding nervous. "But it passed us, and circled, and now it's back. What do you think?"

"I don't know. But I'll bet I have a pretty good idea." I switched sides so I was walking closer to the street. "Let's slow down for a minute."

We walked slowly, me looking at the street out of the corner of my eye, waiting to see if the black car would follow. It did, inching closer behind us on the street. I walked slower and slower, Di keeping the same pace, until the car had no choice but to stop so it wouldn't pass us.

Then I stopped, too, abruptly. I turned to face the street and stared squarely at the passenger window of the car, tinted so black I couldn't see anything but my own scowling face reflected back at me. The window slowly glided down.

Staring back at me from across the console was Mr. White.

"Mr. White," I cried. "What are you doing? Are you following us?"

He looked a little surprised, and opened his mouth to speak, but paused, like he was thinking.

"Look, Mr. White, I know you like to chat, but uh, me and Di have some serious stuff to do, so . . ."

"Also, excuse me," Di said, stepping forward. "But do you know how suspicious what you're doing is?! Driving around following kids in a black car, while wearing a full suit? Why are you being such a creep? Aren't you a *realtor*?"

Mr. White stared at us with his mouth in a tight straight line. He looked like he was going to yell at us, but when he spoke, it was in a calm voice.

"Actually," he said. "I am not a realtor."

Di and I glanced at each other out of the corners of our eyes.

"Um, okay," she said.

"And my name is not Mr. White."

My hand had a mind of its own when it grabbed onto Di's hand. I was getting ready to run. Here was a light-thief, disguised as the guy who'd been helping Mrs. McGee. Right in front of me.

"My name is Agent Watson," he went on. "And I am a representative of the Bureau of Weird Happenings. We're a special, covert organization responsible for protecting citizens from all things weird. It's super top-secret stuff, so you've never heard of us but—"

"Actually, we have heard of BWH," Di interrupted. "Like, just today."

The man in the car looked shocked, and I was shocked, too. Not a light-thief? An agent?

"H-how?" he stammered.

"Chatter," Di said smugly.

"Well, um, okay. I will need to look into that," he said. "But for now. This is urgent. I was assigned to Ferrous City for reasons that are too vast to explain at this moment—"

"Let me guess," Di interrupted again. "You've heard about the threat of an alien invasion."

Agent Watson's jaw dropped.

"How did you . . . ?"

"We live here," I say. "You were just assigned."

"We had intelligence that you were in contact with an alien life-form this summer," he said, trying to get a grip. "At first, we didn't take the threat seriously, so we sent in a couple of junior agents, but they couldn't find anything. But when the life-form was confirmed, they sent me."

"Wait a second!" I yell. "Were these junior agents in gray suits?"

"Yep, that was them," Watson replied.

Di and I give each other a knowing look. This explained so much.

"Well, we were in touch with an alien," I said quickly. "But it's gone now."

All my worries about taking care of Cheese were bubbling inside me like a volcano. I thought about what Jodie said, about agents trying to study Cheese. I wouldn't let that happen.

"We know," Agent Watson said. "But it's not *that* lifeform we're worried about. We're worried about the *other* ones."

"Yeah, us, too," said Di. "Believe me."

"Do you have intelligence about *them*?" I asked. "What are you going to do?"

"From what we understand," Agent Watson said, "they're angry that their scouts were eliminated before delivering their samples from Earth."

"Samples," I said. "You mean stuff that shows their leaders whether they want to, like, colonize us or not? Because that's what they do. They suck the resources out of wherever they go."

"You have a lot of information," Agent Watson said, frowning a little. "Yes, those kinds of samples. We were able to recover one tube from the last site we followed them to, but we haven't been able to find any in Ferrous City. Based on the other sample, it looks like they're gathering things like aloe plants, lavender, chamomile. We believe they must be interested in plants that have soothing, healing properties. They weren't able to give that information back to their leaders. They're sending more scouts to finish the job."

"So, if they get their sample tubes, they'll just go away?" Di said hopefully.

"I wish that were the case," Agent Watson said. "They seem to be after specific resources from different planets. Natural power, medicine, maybe weapons next? Whatever they're preparing for, it's big. They could likely be stocking up for a full-on assault on the galaxy."

We all went silent. The thought of an attack on our planet was heavy.

"Or maybe they just want revenge," I added, trying to change the subject. "Since we . . . eliminated their last scouts."

"*You* eliminated their last scouts?"

He raised his eyebrows.

"Um, it was a busy day," Di said.

"Look," I said. "We don't really have time to go back and forth. We have evidence that says the light-thieves are on their way. And we have a plan to stop them."

"What kind of plan?"

"We're making devices to defend against them. We hope that if we can show the scouts that Earth isn't going to back down, that they'll move on."

"Lord," Agent Watson said. "You kids have been going through a lot."

"Yeah, what's new?" Di said.

"Do you know how you're going to track down the scouts?" Agent Watson asked.

"No," I admitted. "And they could look like anyone. I honestly have no idea how we're going to track them down, other than hoping they come to us."

"I might have something that could help," Agent Watson said. "The Bureau has developed a tool that tracks alien life-forms. It's not perfect, but it's been known to work in a twenty-five-square-mile radius."

The alien material tracker, I thought to myself. Jodie wasn't lying.

"*It's been known to work*," Di said, her eyes widening. "Exactly how many aliens are here every day?"

"That's classified."

"Good grief," she said, covering her face.

"Okay," I said. "If you really want to help, go get the device and you can meet us at Hathaway Park. Maybe between your device and our defense plan, we might have a chance."

"Deal."

"Agent Watson," I said, before he could roll his window up. "The life-form that we had contact with. If you found it, what would you do to it?"

He looked a little puzzled.

"Do to it?" he said. "What do you mean? We wouldn't do anything to it. Our job is to help get them back on track. Supplies, machinery repair, those things."

I nodded, relief flooding through me.

"Why do you ask?" he said.

"Just making sure. Now, we should really hurry up."

Agent Watson nodded and the black car zoomed down the street, leaving me and Di to run the rest of the way to my house. We arrived panting, to find my whole family at home playing Monopoly. They were surprised when I burst into the house with Di behind me, both of us breathing hard.

"Ethan," my mom said. "I was just about to text you. Wow, you're sweaty. Have you been running a marathon? You're just in time to play, if you want. I'm the shoe this time, though, sorry."

"No, thanks, Mom, we're in a rush!" I turned to Di. "You stay down here, I'm going to run up to my room and grab stuff and then we can go."

"Ethan?" my dad said slowly.

"Oh, sorry," I said. "This is Di, everybody. Di, this is my family."

"Hi, nice to meet you," Di said, smiling.

"Oh, it's *Di*," Troy said, grinning hugely. "I know that name."

"You're RJ's sister, aren't you?" my mom said quickly in a friendly voice. "I know your face from the park. Sure you don't want to join us for a game?"

"No, thank you, ma'am," she said. "Ethan's right. We have to hurry."

"Is there something going on?" my dad asked.

"Um, not exactly. Kind of. Just a group project we're working on. Nothing major." I laughed nervously, then turned to Di. "I'll be *right* back."

I dashed up the stairs to my room, then raced around throwing everything that looked like it had defense potential into my backpack. Duct tape. Flashlights. Toothpicks. Nuts and bolts. Wire. By the time I found more stuff, the backpack was bulging. I carried a couple things under my arm and then raced back down the stairs.

"Bye, Nugget! Wish me luck!"

I listened for the squeak Nugget usually makes when he hears his name, but it never came.

"Don't worry, I'll be ba—"

I looked toward Nugget's cage. The door was open with Nugget nowhere in sight.

"Nugget?" I called out.

I walked over to Nugget's cage and my heart sank. My skin heated up and I could feel myself start to sweat.

"Nugget!" I called out again, searching through his cage. A light-thief couldn't have taken him, could it? I didn't even want to consider that possibility. Nugget was crafty, quick even. Surely, he could escape a light-thief.

But the more I thought about it, the more I started to doubt myself.

"Ethan!" my mom called out. "Remember, your friend is waiting!"

"Coming!" I yelled back down. I felt my head about to pop.

Then, like he heard my worried thoughts and decided the game was over, Nugget emerged from under my bed. My whole body relaxed as I raced over to him.

"You've got to be more careful and stay in your cage," I scolded him. "It's the safest place for you right now."

Once Nugget was secure, I picked up my things and raced down the stairs.

"You okay?" Di whispered. She could see my panicked spirit.

"Yeah, just a scare. Let's just get out of here," I whispered back. "We were just talking to Di about school," my mom said. "Apparently, you organized a petition for vegetarian food in the cafeteria! We didn't know about that! Very cool."

I felt my face flushed even more, especially because I could feel my brothers' eyes on me, grinning and waiting to drop a bunch of jokes. I avoided them, pretending they didn't exist.

"It was really nice to know somebody has my back," Di said, smiling.

"Oh, he definitely does," Troy said.

"*Okay*, Di," I said loudly to drown him out. "I think I have everything we need. Let's go."

"Is that a toaster?" my dad saying, eyeing the toaster under my arm.

"Um, yes."

"Why?"

"School project!" I said. We had to get out of here. I grabbed Di's hand and pulled her toward the door. The feeling of her hand in mine made all the noise fall away, just for a moment.

"I'll be back before the streetlights go on," I called to my parents. "Promise."

25

NO IDEA IS BAD

Despite being held up by the confrontation with Agent Watson and being slowed down by my family's need to be nosy, Di and I still got to the park before anyone else. I even stopped by Mrs. McGee's and grabbed Handy-Bot in case we could use the extra arms. I told Mrs. McGee I was taking him to make a few upgrades. A small lie.

But the whole time my mind was on the light-thief as the clouds in the sky grew grayer and grayer. Were we really ready to face it this time? Di could tell my head was somewhere else.

"Ethan," she said softly.

"Huh?" I said, a little startled.

"You can tell me what's wrong, you know."

I didn't have the energy for any more secrets. "I thought I lost Nugget right before this," I said grimly.

"What?" Di sprang up. "What happened?"

"It was fine, he just got out of his cage, but I—what if I can't protect him? Or anyone here?"

I buried my face in my hands, doing my best not to cry in front of Di. The gloomy sky and fog didn't help make me feel any better. Then it started to drizzle.

"It's okay, Ethan," Di said, putting her hand on my shoulder. "It's all going to work out. It always does."

Something about her voice made me believe her. I sat up and brushed it off.

"You're right. Thank you, Di. I'm lucky to have you as a friend."

"Same."

After that we were quiet for a while, staring over at the basketball court where a kid had forgotten a remote-controlled car.

"Your parents are so nice," Di said abruptly. "They really don't mind if you just wander around the city?"

"I mean, they do," I shrugged. "But I think they feel better about it now that I have a phone."

"That helps," she said.

We sit in silence for a minute. Then she turned toward me a little bit.

"You know, I meant what I said. About it being nice to know you have my back."

"I definitely do," I said. I didn't know what else to say, but I meant that part for sure, so I said it again: "I definitely do."

Juan Carlos's voice echoed across the park: "Ethan! Diamond!"

He and Kareem and Fatima appeared at the far edge of Hathaway Park. They were moving toward us at a quick pace, lumbering a little because of the stuff they carried. Di and I both stood to meet them. I was eager to see what they'd found, and I was hoping that with all the stuff I'd brought and all the stuff they'd brought, that we would have *something* we could put together to defeat the light-thief scouts.

If we could even find them.

"Any luck?" Fatima said when they got closer. She was carrying a cardboard box and Kareem and Juan Carlos each did, too. Stuff spilled out of the tops of all three. Odds and ends like you wouldn't believe.

"Not as lucky as y'all," I said, laughing. "We should be able to make something from all *this*."

"We'd better," she said.

"She took a piece of her dad's grill!" Juan Carlos nearly shouted. "And some logs out of her fireplace!"

"*Logs?*" I said.

"They're quick-start fire logs," she said. "I'm pretty sure that means there's a trigger or a switch inside. Could be useful."

"Don't worry," Kareem said. He hoisted a fire extinguisher. "We have safety measures under control."

I was starting to understand how Fatima saw the world, the way pieces of other things fit inside others. Usually, I had to take something apart first to see how it might work with something else, but she had a different kind of imagination. It was cool that she shared it with us.

Wait. Speaking of sharing.

"Okay," I said loudly. "Everything is hectic right now. So, before I forget: Me and Di ran into that realtor dude. Um, turns out he's not a realtor. He's an agent."

"From the Bureau of Weird Happenings," Di added.

"That's *real*?" Juan Carlos cried. "That's such a ridiculous name!"

"Yes." I let it all flood out. "Apparently, they already kind of know about the light-thieves. They've been getting, you know, intelligence or whatever. And he's going to come and help us. He has an alien tracking device thing. And they believe the light-thieves are gathering intel about plants on Earth. Soothing ones like chamomile and stuff. That's part of why the scouts are coming back. To get what the last scouts didn't return with."

"Soothing plants," Fatima said thoughtfully. Again, her brain was cool. Everything I said, and *that* was what she focused on.

"You're sure this guy is cool?" Kareem said skeptically.

"He's cool," Di said. And it was nice to know she had my back, too.

"One thing at a time," Fatima said. "Defense."

We laid everything we had gathered on the picnic table in the shade, then we stood back to survey it all. Kareem cupped his chin in his hand, looking studious. Juan Carlos rested his hands on top of his head. Di had her arms crossed and Fatima pressed the knuckles of each hand against each other. I stood there with my arms hanging at my sides, my head cocked. We were all thinking.

"What if we . . . never mind," Juan Carlos said first.

"No idea is a bad idea at this stage," Fatima said. "Throw it all out there."

"No, really, it was bad," he said, grinning. "I was going to say we could just duct tape lighters to those shish kabob sticks right there."

"Rudimentary doesn't mean bad," Fatima said.

"But let's keep thinking," Di said kindly.

I couldn't believe I wanted to burst out laughing with the stakes as high as they were. I guess this was what happened when you had to save the world with your best friends. And Fatima. Although I guess I considered her a friend now, too.

"Okay," Kareem said, his hands out in front of him like he was about to give a presentation. "We take the bulbs out of the flashlights, and maybe we can figure out how to turn the switch into an on-off device. Like, you know in Britain they call a flashlight a torch? Well, it's like an actual torch, with fire, but we can turn it on and off without having to light it every time, because that's too slow."

Fatima tilted her head sideways, eyebrows raised.

"Not bad at all," she said. "Let's explore the possibilities with that."

We dug through the pile for all the flashlights—there were four.

"Where's that grill?" she said, searching. "Ah, here we go. What if we . . ."

I knew we were in a rush, but none of us wanted to rush the process. Every time we tried something that didn't work, I would turn and sweep my eyes over Hathaway Park, making sure that the scouts weren't sneaking up on us.

"I don't think the torch idea is going to work," Fatima said, sounding disappointed. Kareem looked bummed out, but he nodded.

"We gotta move on to something that will work then," he said. "Who else has an idea?"

We tried turning an umbrella stick into a big lighter. We tried making a catapult, but we figured if we burned down Ferrous City in the process of fighting off the scouts, then we might as well have done the aliens' job for them.

"How did the weapon that Cheese's people used on the light-thieves work?" Di said.

"I don't think we have their kind of resources," Fatima said.

"No," Di said. "But what if we made something that could move? We could use it to chase the light-thief into a position where we could get to it and sneak attack? Or something? Maybe?"

Fatima had a half smile on her face, thinking. "That's a good idea. But what could we use?"

We all eyed the pile of supplies. Lots of different odds and ends, but nothing with wheels. As I looked on the other side on the bench, my eyes widened.

"I know!" I said excitedly. Everyone followed my gaze right to Handy-Bot.

"Ethan, that's perfect," Fatima said. "Yes! This could work. I can use a piece of the start log and attach it to Handy-Bot with—"

"Duct tape," Kareem said. "Ethan uses duct tape for everything."

I shrugged. "Tried and true."

Fatima laughed, and then we got to work.

It was easy once we figured out how the fire-start mechanism worked. It was kind of like a match and the back of a matchbook. With the touch of a button on the remote, the piece of the log on top of Handy-Bot ignited. We only practiced once. We didn't want Handy-Bot to go up in flames.

And then Fatima had another idea. Out of my pile of junk, she withdrew an old Nerf gun.

"Ah!" she said. "What have we here!"

"I figured it was worth bringing," I shrugged.

"It definitely was," she said. "Look at what I'm thinking."

Everyone else stood to watch while Fatima and I leaned over the table and studied what needed to be done to bring her vision to life. A flamethrower, but less potentially cata-strophic. A concentrated stream of fire. Could be good up close. But first we had to get up close. I looked around, wor-ried, wondering when Agent Watson was going to decide to show up. If ever.

"If we can just get this part to connect without flooding the chamber," Fatima muttered, thinking out loud.

"You are so smart," I said. I was almost surprised I said it out loud. But it was on my mind, so it came out. She looked surprised, too. "Like, so, so smart. It's awesome because we're, like, smart in different ways and we see different ways to solve problems and I just wanted you to know I'm really glad you got put in our group. We are lucky."

She smiled the most genuine, friendly smile, and it was a good feeling to have overcome something that seemed so insurmountable in the past. She opened her mouth to respond, but then we heard a voice calling for help.

"Hello? Anybody? I'm lost! Can anybody help me?"

Everyone's head snapped around to look for the source of the voice.

"Anybody? I'm stuck! Help!"

"Stuck where?" Di called, looking concerned. "Where are you?"

"Here! I'm right here!"

Sure enough, over by the basketball court I see a kid. He's taller than I thought he would be. I expected a little boy based on his words. But he was hunched over on the bench. I don't know how I didn't see him before.

"Help," he called. "Please!"

Di took a step forward, but something made me reach out and grab her arm. My stomach felt like it was curling in on itself.

"Wait," I said, at the same time I heard someone calling my name.

"Ethan!" Agent Watson called. I saw him now, coming across the field. He wore black gloves, and in his hands he held something that looked like an hourglass on a stick. "Is everything alright? Have you told your friends that I—"

But then he paused mid-step. He seemed confused, then stopped fully and looked down at the device in his hand. From here, it looked like it was shaking his hand, almost making his whole arm vibrate. And then it started to glow.

"What the . . . ?" he started, but I was already putting it together. My hand was still on Di's arm, and I pulled her back hard.

The alien detector held by Agent Watson was glowing bright red by the time I looked back at the kid on the sidewalk. The kid was standing straight up now, not crouched over anymore. Now I could see his face, and I recognized it.

"Jodie," I said, confused.

"From AHA?" Kareem said.

Jodie was smiling at us. Then he wasn't Jodie anymore. His face slowly began to peel off in gray scales. Agent Watson's eyes got huge. Before he had taken a single step forward, the disguise of Jodie had fully fallen away, and there before us stood a light-thief scout.

26

BLUFFING AND IRRITANTS

Around the picnic table were stones, gray and sharp. Di started throwing them before the scout had taken a single slithering step toward us. The first one connected with its head. The second right in the eye. It hissed and roared, recoiling. Kareem caught on quickly and then he and Juan Carlos started hurling rocks, too. Some missed, but most landed, and the light-thief was surprised by the aggressive onslaught.

"We need fire to make it go away!" Di yelled at me and Fatima. We nodded, and quickly turned back to the picnic table.

"If we can connect the top chamber and the bottom valve, we can make it work!" she cried. "We just have to make sure the switch works without fail or the whole thing will be a waste."

"What if we used a splitter?" I said, frantically digging through the pile of odds and ends. Over my shoulder I heard the light-thief squeal as another of the sharp rocks connected. But it sounded closer. No way rocks could fend it off forever. Fatima and I had to hurry.

"Good idea," she said, grabbing the splitter as soon as I dug it out. We took turns tweaking and turning and grabbing and twisting. Then I heard a scream.

The light-thief was chasing Di. It was hard on her trail and I felt a yell rip out of my throat. I sprinted away from the table after the alien, even though I had no plan whatsoever. Then I remembered the remote control to Handy-Bot.

I wheeled back toward the picnic table and grabbed the control off the picnic table bench, then whirled around and slammed it into gear. Handy-Bot screeched into motion, racing across the field to where the alien was chasing Di. Agent Watson was chasing the light-thief, too, but it didn't seem as if he had a plan, either.

It looked like Di was racing toward the barbecue pits, so I ran after her, steering Handy-Bot ahead of me to stay in its range. I didn't want to ignite it too soon—we hadn't had a chance to test it more than once, so I had no idea how long it would burn. I just hoped it would be long enough.

When Di reached the barbecue pits, I was ten feet behind the alien. Handy-Bot squealed ahead. It was time.

I slammed my thumb on the button we had wired for ignition. A breath later, Handy-Bot burst into flames, and it barreled toward the alien. The scout didn't notice Handy-Bot's approach until it was almost too late.

It leaped out of the way just in time. Handy-Bot slammed into the pole of a rusty grill. Flaming shards scattered everywhere. The alien roared in a high-pitched voice, its eyes going white with terror, backing away clumsily. Di grabbed a few of the pieces of burning material by their edges, throwing them into different grills, where the flames grew. The alien soon found itself surrounded by fire on all sides, roaring as it seemed to shrink a little.

Then it fled the barbecue area, where Di stood in the center, surrounded by the safety of the grills.

"Kareem! Juan Carlos! Go to the grills!" Fatima yelled. "Be safe!"

She was still finishing the weapon at the table. I prayed she was almost done.

I steered what was left of Handy-Bot after the light-thief. The burning robot plunged after it, spinning through the grass. I could tell the flame was getting lower. The threat of our defense was only going to last for a little longer.

Kareem and Juan Carlos followed Fatima's instructions and ran for the barbecue pit. The alien scout saw them as they tried to cut across the field, and it angled toward them, sharp teeth shining and angry.

Then Agent Watson appeared between the alien and my friends, wielding the alien detector. It wasn't a weapon. We all knew this. But Watson held it like it was.

"Stop right there," he called. "Do you see this device? This is a device that, if fired, will attach its frequency to your nervous system and will transmit to your kind. If you leave now, you and your kind may exit our atmosphere in peace. But if you continue on your current course, I will have no choice but to fire. And you know what will happen if I do."

I watched silently. If I didn't know he was bluffing, I would totally think he was telling the truth. He aimed the detector at the light-thief scout with the confidence of a warrior. From the corner of my eye, I saw Fatima dart away from the picnic table toward the forested area by the basketball courts. Was she going to hide? Did the weapon fail? I couldn't follow her. I had to keep my eyes on the light-thief.

"What's your choice?" Agent Watson yelled at the alien.

Like lightning, the alien's huge, clawed arm swung out and knocked the device right out of Agent Watson's hands. It splintered on the ground.

"Where's your real weapon!?" I yelled from my station.

"The agency hasn't issued me one yet!" he yelled, slowly backing away from the alien headed his way. "But don't worry; back up is on the way!"

I shook my head. Backup always takes forever. The alien grinned its horrible smile with its horrible sharp teeth and reached back to swing again.

"Hey, you!" Juan Carlos yelled.

He had left the circle of grills and grabbed one of the modified umbrellas. They may not have been the cleanest attempt at an invention, but clean was out the window right now. We needed *anything* and Juan Carlos knew it.

He scraped the altered umbrella's tip across the rough pavement and the fire immediately sprang to life. The scout saw it out of the corner of its eye and whirled on him, but Juan Carlos was already waving the umbrella stick in its eyes and face, watching it recoil even as it bared its teeth.

Out of the corner of my eye I saw Agent Watson sprint to grab another one. *No weapons, and weak defense. What were we going to do?*

"Leave this planet," Agent Watson shouted, waving the burning umbrella close to the alien's face.

The light-thief didn't budge.

"Is this what you're looking for?" called a voice. We all jerked our heads (even the light-thief) toward the sound.

It was Jodie. The real Jodie. Standing next to Fatima. Jodie held something high in the air over his head.

The light-thief hissed.

"That's right," Fatima said. "We recovered your samples. This is what you wanted, right? Samples to show your boss? To decide whether Earth is worth the trouble? Well, here you go. Take it."

Agent Watson and Juan Carlos continued holding the fiery umbrellas up, but the fire was getting low. The light-thief wasn't focused on them anymore. It was focused on Fatima.

"Fatima, be careful," I called.

"I know what I'm doing," she said evenly. "Jodie, give our friend here the samples."

Jodie looked completely unfazed to be walking toward an alien. I guess, based on his obsession with aliens, this was probably the high point of his life. He held two tubes, one in each hand. When he reached the alien, he held them out calmly. The tubes had a venting apparatus on top.

The alien's claw extended toward Jodie, and my whole body tensed. But the claw plucked each tube from Jodie hands, and then backed away. It smiled its usual hideous smile, then cracked open one of the tubes.

A gross skinny tentacle emerged from its face and slithered down into the tube.

Then everything got loud.

The alien screeched, like it was being burned. Fatima grabbed Jodie and they sprinted toward the grills. I sprinted after them, not knowing what else to do. Juan Carlos beat me there by two steps.

Both tubes were open, a tentacle in each one, and the alien was writhing and screeching even louder than before.

Its face turned gray, the scales all looking ashy. It seemed to swell, ballooning hideously. We all watched in horror.

Then it burst.

It sounded like a watermelon thrown from a third-story window. We ducked behind the grills as slime splattered everywhere. When I peeked out again, all that remained was a worm-like creature in the center of the mess. Its eyes glowed red. It crawled a few inches toward one of the tubes, started to glow, and then both the worm and the tube disappeared.

"What . . . what just happened?" Agent Watson said. He hadn't ducked in time. He and the no-longer-burning umbrella were doused in goo.

"That was awesome!" Kareem yelled. "What was that?"

"Jodie found the light-thieves' tubes," Fatima said, standing up. She flicked a spot of slime off her shoulder. "I ran into him in the trees when I went to grab samples. The plan kind of made itself."

"I told you I'd find evidence," Jodie said. He was grinning but he also looked stunned, like he was floating on cloud nine.

"What samples? What plan?" I cried.

"The fire weapon wasn't going to work," Fatima said. "Weapons usually don't, I realized. They solve a problem but usually create more. Then I remembered what you said Agent Watson told you about the light-thieves looking for soothing plants as samples. So, I, well . . . I decided to give them samples. Just not soothing ones."

"What was in those tubes?" Di cried.

"Poison ivy," Fatima grinned. "And ragweed. Both different kinds of irritants. I saw tons of it down by Gadget Beach and figured there'd be some here in these woods, too. I was right."

"It . . . it worked," Watson said. "I can't believe it worked. If that's the intelligence they take back to their superiors, there's no way they'll be back. I can't believe it."

"I can," I said. "Fatima did it."

"So it's gone?" Kareem said slowly.

"It certainly seems to be," Agent Watson said. It's like he didn't even mind being covered in alien slime. "That little worm was all that was left, and it's going to report back now."

"We have a pretty good record," Juan Carlos said. "Three–zero in obliterating light-thieves."

"Well, *we* didn't exactly obliterate it," Kareem said. "Technically."

"This was even better," Watson said. "You kids have a career at the BWH if you want one."

"Man, you might as well give us badges now," Kareem said haughtily. We all cracked up. It was like a pressure valve releasing all the fear and tension.

"I'll certainly be calling on you for advice," Watson said humbly. "The kids of Ferrous City know a lot about aliens."

"Are you serious?" Jodie said. "Like for real? Can we seriously have a badge, though? Can I ask you some questions?"

"I wish you could, but it's probably best if you kids leave this area now," Watson said. "The clean-up team from the Bureau is going to be coming in soon, and I want to keep you all out of this. I will be speaking to my team about all of you, though. I assure you there will be thanks coming your way. We will cover for you however necessary."

"Thanks, Agent Watson," I said. I stepped carefully over the pile of gray ash that fell in the shape of the light-thief scout.

"We'll be keeping an eye on Ferrous City," he said. "Now that we know where to look. If there are any weird happenings, the Bureau will be around."

"You guys really need a different name," Juan Carlos grumbled.

NEW BEGINNINGS

The thing about guinea pigs was that they know when you're feeling worried.

At least, Nugget does.

I sat on the floor of my very clean room, looking around at all the work I'd spent the afternoon doing. When I'd asked my mom if she'd buy me some plastic bins to get everything organized, she'd looked shocked but didn't ask any questions. Then I'd spent hours getting everything in my room/workshop off the floor and into bins. My brain might not have been as organized as Fatima's—we were different people with different ways of thinking—but now my room was, and I realized I could probably think better if everything wasn't so cluttered.

When I was done, though, I realized that I'd been keeping busy but it didn't make me feel any less worried. That was when Nugget crawled out of the shoe he'd been napping in and over to my lap, climbing up. His little warm body was comforting as I stroked his back.

"What if it does come back?" I asked him, just to get the thoughts out of my head. "What if there are tons of them? Not just in Ferrous City, but all around Earth?"

It was the kind of question I didn't want to ask my friends because the idea of worrying them when they were having a good day made me feel sad. I felt the heaviness weighing down on my shoulders. What if, what if, what if . . . the pressure of finding solutions.

But then I remembered what Troy said, what I'd seen in action. That sharing the weight was the only way to feel relief.

I reached for my phone, trying not to disturb Nugget, and sent a text into the now-expanded group text.

Me: *Hey what's everybody doing? Can anybody meet up at Hathaway? I need to talk to y'all.*

I sat and waited as the answers rolled in.

Fatima: *Sorry, I'm right in the middle of wiring a solar panel.*

Kareem: *Can't. I'm babysitting.*

Juan Carlos: *Helping my abuela with a church thing, sorry!*

I sighed. Sharing the weight of the world would have to wait. Then the last text came in.

Di: *I can meet. Wanna walk over there now?*

The park was just as empty as it was the day we defeated the light-thief scout. In some ways it looked exactly the same, minus piles of alien goo. The Bureau of Weird Happenings had been very thorough in their clean-up efforts. As I walked over to the same picnic table, I imagined them squeegeeing the goo into a zip-top evidence bag, taking it somewhere and looking at it under a microscope. I was a little jealous thinking about that. Maybe instead of *just* being an inventor when I grew up, I could work there. I wondered where *there* was. Probably in a random building that looked like it did computer repairs or something.

"Hey," Di called when she arrived. She was coming from the direction of the barbecue area. I remembered how worried I'd been when the light-thief was chasing her. When she reached me, she looked down at the scorch mark on the pavement nearby, the only thing left of what had happened with the alien scout.

"So weird to think it was just a week ago," she said.

"It feels like a long time ago and yesterday at the same time," I said. "I can't believe we've fought light-thieves twice and it's not even winter."

"I hope winter is a lot more boring," she said, and we both laughed before she said: "Have you talked to Cheese?"

"Yeah, we talked," I said. "My buddy and its family are doing okay. They haven't had any more run-ins with the light-thieves. But that's why I texted the group. I'm worried. What if there are more? What if they're just lying low?"

Di shrugged.

"My granny always says, 'A what-if never made a sandwich.'" She laughed. "I think it means you have to worry about it when it happens. Waiting for bad stuff to happen just means you're not enjoying when bad stuff isn't happening."

"True," I said. "But there's something to be said for being prepared."

"I think a place like Ferrous City is going to be prepared no matter what," she said. "With us here."

Something about the way she said *us* made my face flush.

"You know," I said, staring down at the ground. "I'm glad we became friends. I know we weren't, really. Not before this summer."

"Yeah, well, sometimes it takes something big to bring people together."

We were both staring at the ground, but I snuck a glance at her. It turned out she was sneaking a glance at me at the same time.

"I don't want to be weird," I said. "But I think I like you."

"What kind of *like* me?"

"You know. I *like* you."

She pretended to pick something off her pants.

"Okay, well I *like you* like you, too."

Neither of us looked at each other, but I was smiling and I could see her smiling out of the corner of my eye. When both our phones went off, I was kind of annoyed that something was interrupting what felt like the coolest thing ever.

But I wasn't annoyed once I read the text. We each stared at our phones, eyes huge.

Juan Carlos: *GUYS my parents passed their citizenship test! With flying colors. I feel like I could take off flying.*

Di and I were sitting right next to each other, but we wrote back anyway:

Me: *JUAN CARLOS, THIS IS THE BEST THING EVER!*

Di: *Your parents deserve this and more! We need to celebrate!*

The sun was setting, and I had no idea what was going to happen in the future, but Di's grandmother was right about worrying and sandwiches. I tried to exist right here on this planet, in this moment. We were sitting in the same place a week ago, when it seemed like the world was lost. Now, it seemed like the world was just beginning.

EPILOGUE

I headed back to my house, taking a second to really look at it. We're not moving. None of my friends are leaving, either. After the battle with the light-thief, I almost didn't realize how relieved I was to know that.

I padded my way back up to my bedroom, careful to not disturb any of my family. The last thing I need is to have to give anyone a full alien debrief. But I had other things to attend to then.

"Cheese and crackers."

The flower phone activated and the fuchsia light told me I could send my video.

"Hey, buddy, guess what? Fatima has been helping me work on getting patented. We're all still working on our big group project, trying to find other ways to communicate with our friends in space. It's a lot easier doing science stuff with her when I'm not trying to be better than her. In some ways I'm better *with* her, you know? We make a great team.

I have this machine that I'm working on, but I'm starting to get interested in solutions. Your light-flowers inspired me. I want to figure out how to make things grow, like I was doing before. And Fatima loves focusing on solar power. How cool is that? Anyway, it's looking like my device is going to be patented, and we're having a party next week to celebrate. I wish you were here. I hope everything is okay. Here's a song by Stevie Wonder. Hopefully this will help you understand what I'm feeling. Send message."

I flopped back on my bed after sending the message. Sometimes I wished I could tell my family about Cheese. They would love to hear about the adventures Cheese shares with me. Just last week I got a video of Cheese flying through a meteor shower. The ship has shields that make it safe to fly through meteor showers. It was amazing to watch. The kind of thing that more people should see. I imagined the scientists at NASA losing their minds about the kind of footage I saw from Cheese.

I got a response from Cheese. *That was quick!*

"Ethan," he said when the image of him materialized. He spun to show me his excitement. It was so cool hearing him learn to speak our language. Then he showed me a light-picture. It was of a window, and a night sky. An image of Cheese pointing at it.

Confused, I stared at the video for a second after the image of Cheese disappeared. Then I slowly turned my head to face my window.

Outside in the dark, far out into the neighborhood, just above Hathaway Park, two bright lights, green and blazing, arced down from the sky.

"Is that . . . ?" I whispered. "Nugget, you have to see this!"

I turned to Nugget's cage, ready to investigate with him.

It was open.

My heart shot up to my throat.

The cage door was open and there was no Nugget inside. While my muscles itched to run around my room and tear it apart, one detail settled in my stomach like a radioactive rock.

There was goo in Nugget's cage. The same kind as the light-thieves leave. Agent Watson had mentioned scouts, plural, but we had only defeated one. The other one had— oh no—

We might've won the battle, but they weren't done fighting.

They'd kidnapped Nugget.

ACKNOWLEDGMENTS (TK)

ABOUT THE AUTHOR

Nick Brooks is an award-winning filmmaker and writer. His short film *Hoop Dreamin'* earned him the George Lucas Scholar Award and was a finalist in the Forbes 30 Under 30 Film Fest. His short film *Bee* won the James Bridges and Jack Larson Award for Writing and Directing and premiered at the American Black Film Festival. He is the author of *Promise Boys* and *Nothing Interesting Ever Happens to Ethan Fairmont*. Nick lives in Los Angeles, California; he's originally from Washington, DC. Visit Nick at thenickbrooks.com.